ALSO BY
DARCY COATES

The Haunting of Ashburn House
The Haunting of Blackwood House
The House Next Door
Craven Manor
The Haunting of Rookward House
The Carrow Haunt
Hunted
The Folcroft Ghosts
The Haunting of Gillespie House
Dead Lake
Parasite
Quarter to Midnight
Small Horrors

House of Shadows
House of Shadows
House of Secrets

Black Winter
Voices in the Snow
Secrets in the Dark

HOUSE

OF

SHADOWS

DARCY COATES

Poisoned Pen
PRESS

Published by Poisoned Pen Press, an imprint of Sourcebooks
P.O. Box 4410, Naperville, Illinois 60567-4410
(630) 961-3900
sourcebooks.com

Originally self-published in 2016 by Black Owl Books.

Library of Congress Cataloging-in-Publication Data
Names: Coates, Darcy, author.
Title: House of shadows / Darcy Coates.
Description: Naperville, Illinois : Poisoned Pen Press, [2020] |
    "Originally self-published in 2016 by Black Owl Books."
Identifiers: LCCN 2019056936 | (trade paperback)
Subjects: GSAFD: Ghost stories.
Classification: LCC PR9619.4.C628 H69 2020 | DDC 823/.92--dc23
LC record available at https://lccn.loc.gov/2019056936

Printed and bound in the United States of America.
VP 10 9 8 7 6 5

CHAPTER 1
THE STRANGER

SOPHIE COULDN'T STOP WATCHING the tall, black-haired man.

The opera had not long finished, and the theater's foyer was filled with some of the most elegant people Sophie had ever seen. Everywhere she looked gave her a new sight: silk, chiffon, and lace dresses shimmered in the candlelight. Decadent flower-and-feather head wear bobbed as the ladies moved through the crowds. All around her was a cacophony of laughing voices and eager conversation. And yet, in the busy room, one person commanded Sophie's attention.

He stood nearly a head above the patrons surrounding him, and his long, pale face contrasted strikingly with eyes so dark they could have been black. He seemed to have stepped out of a colder, grimmer world. If he'd enjoyed the opera, he didn't show it. Sophie thought he must have been searching for something; he stood at the base of the stairs, scanning the crowd, his restless eyes skipping from silk-clad guest to silk-clad guest, until they landed on Sophie and her uncle.

Sophie looked away as a flush of embarrassment rose across her face. *Did he see you staring? You should know better!*

Her Uncle Phillip, who had stopped to greet a friend, waved his companion off and turned to Sophie. "Well then, how did you enjoy the show?"

It was the third time he'd asked, but Sophie replied just as enthusiastically as she had the first time. "It was beautiful! I've had a wonderful night. Thank you."

Her uncle's substantial chest swelled, and he beamed at her. Sophie loved his visits; he was a kind, generous man who liked to indulge her and her siblings whenever he could. Her own father preferred spending his evenings at home, so the opera had become a rare treat since her mother had passed away shortly after Sophie's debut.

Her uncle was on the verge of saying more, but then his eyes rose toward someone behind Sophie's shoulder, and a broad grin bristled his mustache. "Well, Mr. Argenton, I wasn't expecting to see you here! How did you like the show?"

An instinctive part of Sophie knew whom her uncle was addressing even before she turned. The tall, captivating man towered above them. His cheeks seemed a little gaunter at a close distance, and his eyes were dark enough to match his pitch-black hair. Sophie tried to guess his age; she thought he must be close to thirty.

The man inclined his head toward Sophie's uncle and said,

with a voice as clear and cold as winter air, "Very well. Thank you, sir."

"Excellent, excellent. It was a superb show." Her uncle patted his pocket watch absent-mindedly as he spread his smile on both of his companions. "Have you met my niece, Miss Hemlock, yet?"

Mr. Argenton's eyes turned to Sophie. They held her gaze then flicked to her hair for a split second before returning to her face. "I'm afraid I haven't had the pleasure. Miss Hemlock." He bowed, and Sophie returned the gesture.

She was used to her hair drawing attention. It was long, fine, and almost pale enough to be white. Her father had convinced her to wear it in a simple open style with small flowers woven through it, but she was beginning to think that had been a mistake. Even in the foyer packed with showy gowns and glittering, feathered headdresses, her hair drew too much attention. She wished she'd covered it.

"Mr. Argenton imports," Sophie's uncle continued happily. "He's had several joint projects with your father."

"I came to inquire after Mr. Hemlock, in fact. Is he presently at home?" Mr. Argenton faced Sophie's uncle, but his eyes lingered on Sophie.

She tried to smile. His scrutiny made her feel clammy and uncomfortable, but she didn't want to appear rude—especially if Mr. Argenton had business dealings with her father.

"At home, for the time, though I believe he's planning to travel out of town next week." Sophie's uncle, oblivious to his companion's divided attention, continued to beam and pat his pocket watch. "Will you be in town for long, sir?"

"Not for long, no." Mr. Argenton's gaze finally left Sophie to settle back on her uncle.

Sophie let her smile fade. There was something strangely, unsettlingly intense about the man. He was cultured and polite, but she thought there were subtle hints—the slight inflection in his voice and the intense edge to his eyes—that suggested he was capable of terrible, dangerous things. *A sleeping wolf.* She was suddenly grateful to be surrounded by company, even though the theater was quickly emptying.

"I was hoping to visit Mr. Hemlock before I return home," Mr. Argenton continued. "Perhaps tomorrow, if it's convenient."

"Yes, yes, I'm sure it would be. I know he has plans in the morning, but he should certainly be available after three." Uncle Phillip seemed in the mood to continue talking, but Mr. Argenton bowed before his companion could move to a new subject.

"Good evening, sir." He nodded to Sophie. "Miss Hemlock."

Sophie bowed in reply and felt the tension in her shoulders relax as the tall, mysterious Mr. Argenton moved through the lingering guests and toward the street entrance.

"Well, well, fancy meeting him here," Phillip said, more to himself than to her. "Such an odd fellow. I was starting to think he'd never leave that house of his. Well now. Did you enjoy the show?"

Sophie found it more difficult to fill her voice with enthusiasm after being pinned in place by the dark eyes. Still, she managed to praise the singers enough to make her uncle swell happily as he fished his pocket watch out. He took one look at the time, gave a shocked little scoff, and offered his arm to Sophie. "I wasn't expecting us to be this late. I'd better get you home before your father has me shot."

Sophie laughed at that. She let her uncle lead her onto the busy main street, to a row of coaches waiting to ferry their charges across the city.

She was already intending to be out of the house well before Mr. Argenton's visit.

CHAPTER 2
AN UNWELCOME GUEST

ALL OF SOPHIE'S PLANS were foiled.

Despite having been told to come at three, Mr. Argenton rode up to their home not long after one. It was unforgivably early; Sophie had only just changed into her afternoon half-dress, and her father hadn't returned from his appointment with their lawyer.

Sophie had intended to return a visit to one of her friends. It was a long walk and would have easily kept her out until five. She'd hoped Mr. Argenton would have paid his visit and safely departed by then.

Instead, the housemaid brought Sophie his card while another maid was fixing her hair. Sophie tried not to look shocked as she read it.

"I explained Mr. Hemlock was presently out," the housemaid, Anne, said with a small curtsy. "The gentleman said he would be glad to pay his respects to you."

"Oh." Sophie sucked a deep breath in through her nose and straightened her shoulders. "I'll be down in a moment."

She'd taken on the role of hostess of the house twelve months before. She tried her hardest to do the job with as much grace as her mother had, but she knew there was no comparison. Her mother—always kind, always with a clever or insightful remark ready to break through awkward pauses—had made enough friends in the city to fill a theater. In stark contrast, Sophie mishandled more situations than she saved.

"You'll get better with practice," her father had said one evening as he read a book at the dinner table. "You just need to give people a chance to know you."

Sophie looked down at her simple pale-blue dress. The comfortable outfit was meant for a visit to a close friend, not to impress anyone. *It makes me look childish.* There wasn't any time to change, so Sophie sucked in a breath and stood, squeezing her trembling fingers into fists.

You'll be fine. Talk about the poor weather we've been having. Ask him how his trip was. He won't stay for more than fifteen minutes, surely.

She left her bedroom and pressed her back to the wall as her younger brother, Thomas, chased their sister Lucy down the hallway, waving a bug at her. Lucy shrieked with laughter and darted into one of the guest rooms. Their governess gave an apologetic smile as she followed in their wake, and Sophie cringed as Thomas slammed the door. The walls were thin; Mr. Argenton had certainly heard. The noise wouldn't have bothered

7

her so much with any other guest, but Mr. Argenton had radiated such a cool dignity the night before that it almost felt like a sin to disturb his tranquility.

She fought to keep the embarrassed blush off her face as she took the stairs to the ground floor. She paused with her hand on the sitting room's cool brass door handle and took a moment to fix what she hoped was a gracious smile onto her face before entering.

Mr. Argenton stood in front of the window, examining the busy street outside. He seemed even taller inside their home, giving Sophie the impression that their ceiling had been accidentally built a foot too low. He wasn't a large man, but his leanness didn't make him seem weak, either. On the contrary, his pose radiated quiet strength. He turned when he heard the door open, and a faint smile flickered over his lips.

"Miss Hemlock, I hope you're well today."

Sophie gave a small bow. She desperately hoped he wouldn't notice how shaky it was. "I am. Thank you. I'm afraid my father is out, and isn't expected to return for another hour at least."

"That's no concern." His crisp voice was entirely devoid of warmth and life. "I had business near your home and thought it might be a pleasant diversion to sit with you until your father's return."

It wasn't to be a brief visit, after all. Sophie prayed her father would arrive quickly to save her. She indicated to a spare seat and sat opposite. Mr. Argenton crossed his legs and rested his top hat on his knee as his dark eyes skimmed over his host. Once again,

Sophie felt faintly embarrassed by her dress. *I should have worn the maroon pattern instead.*

Her mouth was dry, and she wet her lips before speaking. "Can I offer you some tea?"

"Thank you, but I'm fine."

She nodded and cast around for a safe, easy subject. "Are you planning to be in town for long?"

"Not at all." A hint of faint amusement lingered around his otherwise-bleak eyes. "I came to acquire some furniture for my house; that's all."

"Mr. Johnson in West End has an excellent range—"

"Mr. Johnson's furniture is suited to comfortable homes, such as this one," Mr. Argenton interjected. "I'm afraid it would look sadly out of place at Northwood."

Sophie scrambled to find something to say in reply, but all she managed was, "Oh." Under Mr. Argenton's disconcerting gaze, she felt vulnerable and weak—a lamb sat before a wolf—as though the civility could be dropped at any second and replaced with a danger she couldn't have imagined in her darkest dreams.

Mr. Argenton inclined his head slightly, as though he knew his reply had been too harsh. "Though Mr. Johnson certainly is an excellent woodworker."

Realizing she'd lost her smile, Sophie forced it back onto her face. "Yes, of course. I…" She'd lined up a list of subjects before leaving her room, hadn't she? There'd been something about the weather. Why couldn't she remember even one of them?

"You have younger siblings," Mr. Argenton observed, saving Sophie from the silence.

"Y-yes," she stammered, heat flooding her face again. *Should I apologize?* "Two sisters and a brother."

"I was an only child. I sometimes wonder how different things might have been with siblings."

There was nothing to say to that. Sophie searched for another safe subject. "What part of the country is your house in, sir?"

"A part not many people are familiar with. It's beyond Garlow Town and nearly entirely surrounded by woods. My ancestors didn't make the best choice in location, I'm afraid. Do you like it here?"

The question caught Sophie off guard. "Yes. I've always loved the city. That is—the country is beautiful, too—"

That secretive little smirk was back. "Some of it, certainly."

"Do you live alone?"

"No, my uncle, aunt, and cousin stay with me. Though I'll admit it offers somewhat limited society. None of them play, for instance." He nodded toward the grand piano nestled in the room's corner. "Do you?"

"Ah, yes. A little—"

His dark eyes fixed on hers. They were so intense that Sophie felt the hairs rise on the backs of her arms. "I'd like to hear you, sometime," he said.

A door slammed, and Sophie gasped. She thought it might have been Thomas and Lucy again, but then she heard her father muttering to himself as he shed his coat. Relief at being rescued from the uncomfortable meeting washed through her.

"Sophie?" her father called, his feet clicking on the tile foyer as he crossed to the sitting room. "Are you in here? Ah—" He broke off as he entered the room and caught sight of Mr. Argenton. Sophie felt a chill run through her at her father's face. It was blanched white, and he looked a full five years older than he had when he'd left that morning. She rose from her seat, and Mr. Argenton followed smoothly.

"Pardon the intrusion, sir," Mr. Argenton said, stepping forward. "I was hoping I could speak with you."

A myriad of emotions quickly replaced the shock on her father's face. Sophie saw confusion, frustration, and reluctance. He looked as though he would have given anything to excuse himself, but there was no polite way to avoid the meeting. "Yes. Of course. Would you follow me to my study?"

"I think I might take you up on that offer of tea," Mr. Argenton said to Sophie as he passed her.

She nodded mutely as the door closed behind the gentlemen. Feeling a confusing and alarming mix of sensations, she wrapped her arms around her torso. Mixed into the adrenaline of a danger narrowly escaped was a small hint of euphoria. It was the same rush that made an emboldened man poke at the lion's cage for a second time.

As small and frightened as she felt in Mr. Argenton's presence, Sophie realized she found him strangely fascinating. She would have hated to have sat with him for longer, but conversely, she was disappointed that their conversation had been cut short.

Her mind turned to the interruption—her father. He'd been

agitated and had sought her out as soon as he'd arrived home. *Is something wrong? Has he heard bad news?*

Her father had recently invested in a large shipment of silks from France. It was the sort of import he would have normally split with one or more business partners, but his companion had pulled out at the last minute, leaving him with full ownership of the trade. He'd said he had never before invested such a large amount in a single order. *Nothing could have gone wrong there, could it?*

Sophie remembered that Mr. Argenton had requested tea. Shaking off her stupor, she hurried from the room to find a maid to pass instructions on to, then retired to the library to wait for their visitor to leave.

It wasn't a short wait. Mr. Argenton and Mr. Hemlock remained in the study for more than three hours.

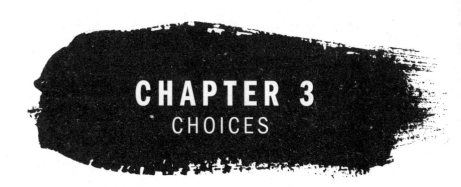

CHAPTER 3
CHOICES

SOPHIE STOOD WHEN SHE heard the study door open. She stayed in the library and listened at the lock as Mr. Argenton crossed the foyer and left their home with brisk, even steps. Once she was sure he was gone, Sophie went into the foyer and waited for her father.

He didn't leave his study for several long minutes, and when he came out, he looked like a changed man.

Sophie hurried to him and put her arm through his to support him. "What's wrong? Are you unwell?"

He opened his mouth but didn't speak. Sophie had the impression there were so many things to say that they all collided on his tongue and choked him. At last, he said, "Come into the study, my dear. Summon some fresh tea."

Sophie sat on the guest's side of the desk. Her father first went to the decanter and poured himself a large glass of brandy. That worried her; Mr. Hemlock never drank before dinner. He then sat next to Sophie, in the second guest chair, rather than in his usual seat behind the desk.

He stared into his glass without speaking for a long time. The maid arrived with a tray of tea, and Sophie poured two cups. Once the maid had left and the door was safely closed, Mr. Hemlock said, "I've made a terrible mess of things, Sophie."

There was nothing she could say, but she leaned closer to encourage him.

"I thought I was being clever. I knew there would be risks, but the rewards would have been so great that I was willing to take the gamble. And now I'm tasting a very, very bitter defeat." He sighed, drained his glass in one swallow, and set it aside. "We've lost the silks. It was foggy last night, the Victor Isle lighthouse keeper became drunk and forgot to refill the lamp's oil, and the ship ran aground on the rocks. Two lives lost…as well as all the cargo."

Sophie knit her hands together. She wished she could say something—anything—to help, but her father wasn't looking at her, and he seemed to want to talk uninterrupted.

"I think I told you that our co-investor pulled out shortly before the order was finalized. I took up his share of the order, which was a substantial amount more than I've ever invested before. But the silks were a good quality at an excellent price, and the turnover would have set us up comfortably for quite a few years."

"How much?" Sophie asked.

Her father finally raised his eyes to meet hers. They looked weaker than she'd ever seen them. "It's not *everything* we own, but it was a large enough sum that it may as well have been."

Sophie let her breath out and focused on her hands. "What does that mean for us?"

"We have enough to hold us for a few more months, but we would need to give up this house. We may be able to afford a smaller place in the country, but the comforts we're used to—the carriage, the maids, the cook—will be too extravagant to keep."

Thomas, who was eight, had been enrolled in an excellent boarding school for the following year. Sophie hardly dared ask what would happen about it. "Thomas's schooling—"

"No, even if we tightened our belts to the point of starvation, we wouldn't be able to afford a full education for him. He will have to be raised as a farmer."

"A farmer!"

Her father bowed his head. "I'm afraid there's no chance of pulling our situation back without assistance, my dear. We don't have enough to invest in a new import—let alone to wait for it to arrive and sell. We are effectively half a step above poverty."

Sophie sat back in the chair. She felt dizzy, and the candles seemed too bright. Thomas's face rushed through her mind, grubby from poking around the library's dusty upper shelves, as he'd proudly announced that he would be a lawyer. There was no longer any hope for that—or for Sophie's two sisters to make a good match when they came of age. They would either become governesses—if a family would take them—or marry other farmers.

Her mind flitted to Mr. Argenton and how insistent he'd been to see Mr. Hemlock. *He works as a merchant, too. Did he hear the news? Did he come to offer sympathy or advice?*

"That brings me to the second issue," Mr. Hemlock said, almost as though he had read Sophie's mind. "Mr. Argenton."

She felt too weak to sit upright, but managed to raise her head to look at her father. "Yes? Did he offer assistance?"

There was a very long pause. "In a way." Sophie's father stood, carried his glass back to the decanter, and refilled it generously. As he poured the brown liquid, he asked, "How well do you know Mr. Argenton?"

"Not well. We met last night at the opera; Uncle Phillip introduced us. And we spoke for perhaps twenty minutes before you came home."

"Well…" Mr. Hemlock leaned against the desk, glass clutched in one hand, and shook his head. There was a bitter smile on his face. It was the sort of smile that a person wears when life is so cruel that there's nothing left to do except laugh at it. "He certainly makes his mind up quickly."

"Father?"

"Mr. Argenton has asked for your hand in marriage."

Sophie frowned. She couldn't decide if she'd misheard or if her father was joking.

"Laugh if you want," Mr. Hemlock said then sipped at his drink. "I almost did when he first proposed it. But I can assure you, he's serious. He wants you to be his wife."

"No," Sophie said, feeling a bemused smile creep across her face. "You're joking. Either you are, or he's joking."

"I don't think he knows how to."

Her smile faltered. "He truly—"

"Asked to marry you, yes. I didn't give him an answer, of course, but he will need one promptly."

"What… Why…why on earth would he want *me*?"

Sophie's father quirked an eyebrow. "Apparently, he likes your hair."

"*My hair?*"

"Men have married for sillier reasons."

Sophie sat forward and covered the lower half of her face with clasped hands. Her, married to Mr. Argenton? It was beyond ridiculous. If he was truly serious, she would have to reject him immediately.

"I'm not going to insist—or even encourage—your decision either way," Mr. Hemlock said before pausing to take another drink.

Sophie thought he was choosing his words carefully.

"But, my dear, I wish you to understand what this proposal means. Mr. Argenton is a very, very wealthy man. He's done incredibly well for himself in the import business; he always seems to buy just the right shipments at precisely the right time. He's either the luckiest human on earth or the smartest. I suspect it's a mix of both."

Wealth. The one thing we desperately need. "If I were to marry him…what would that mean for you? For Thomas and Lucy and Bella?"

Her father shook his head. "Truthfully, I'm not entirely sure.

He said it would be in his power to make reparations for the lost shipment. I'm not sure I believe him. It's a very significant amount of money—I doubt I would even trust a man who was violently in love to keep that kind of promise. And yet, that's what he offered."

Sophie stared at her folded hands. If Mr. Argenton kept his word…if her father and siblings could be returned to their fortunes…

"Putting us aside, I would like you to consider his offer, even just for yourself. You would be mistress of what is, by all accounts, a magnificent house. You would have status and wealth and be established in a higher society."

Sophie opened her mouth, but her thoughts couldn't be expressed in words.

"My dear." Her father's voice was both gentle and sad. "I wish I had managed our finances better. I wish you were still in the position to marry for love. But I'm afraid, now…"

"Yes," Sophie said. She felt numb. No decent, respectable man would want a woman with no dowry or title and whose relatives were reduced to poverty. No man except for Mr. Argenton, apparently. "Is he really serious?"

"It took quite a while for him to convince me, but I believe he is."

"And he understands our situation?"

"He persuaded me to give him a full account. He knows you have no inheritance."

Sophie shook her head. Everything she knew and everything

she was comfortable with had all disappeared in the span of ten minutes. It was so abrupt that she almost felt as though she and her father were discussing a stranger's future. "I still can't understand. If he's that wealthy, he could have almost any girl in the country. Why me?"

"I truly have no idea. Perhaps he wishes to marry quickly and produce an heir for his estate. Or maybe he believes his personality would make it impossible to secure a lady's affections. I'm sure you've noticed—he is quite startling when you first meet him." Mr. Hemlock drained the last of his brandy, set aside the glass, then sat back in the chair opposite Sophie. She chewed on her lower lip, grateful that her father let her think in silence. "Do you know much about him?"

"Almost nothing. His house is a fair way from any town, and while it's supposed to be the most breathtaking building in that part of the country, very few people see it. He doesn't entertain much. Though that's liable to change after he's married."

"And his personality? Is he a kind man?"

"I can't say either way. He's fair and intelligent, but even when we've received shipments under the same account, most of our communication has been through letter. Though I can vouch that his handwriting is straight and neat, just the way it should be."

Sophie managed to chuckle.

Her father, smiling, took both of her hands in his. "My dear, this is your choice, and your choice alone. I swear I will love you just as dearly no matter which path you take."

She stared at her father's hands. They were aging; he wasn't as young or fit as she remembered him. These later years of his life should have been dedicated to comfort and enjoyment, not the grueling, taxing life of a farmworker. She knew he would work hard to keep food on the table and shelter over their heads...but it was in her power to ensure he never had to. And Thomas, dear clever Thomas, could attend his school and become a lawyer. Lucy and Bella would grow up among their peers and enjoy equal society and a good education.

"This is your choice," Mr. Hemlock repeated.

Sophie squeezed his hands back, too overwhelmed to speak.

CHAPTER 4
THE WEDDING

Fifteen days later

"WILT THOU HAVE THIS woman to be thy wedded wife, to live together after God's ordinance in the holy estate of matrimony? Wilt thou love her, comfort her, honor, and keep her in sickness and in health; and, forsaking all others, keep thee only unto her, so long as ye both shall live?"

Mr. Argenton's eyes were darker than night as they fixed on Sophie. "I will."

She knew her hands were shaking. She was sure he could feel it, even through her glove. The priest nodded solemnly then turned to Sophie and began repeating her share of the vows.

Barely sixteen days have passed since I first met him, fifteen since I accepted his proposal. Has there ever been such a short engagement before?

Mr. Argenton had insisted on a quick wedding. He wouldn't be able to stay in the city for long, he'd said, and didn't know when he would return. The implications weren't lost on Sophie—if Mr. Argenton didn't expect to visit the city anytime soon, how long would it be before she saw her family again? Years?

The priest had finished and paused for Sophie's answer. She glanced to her right. It was a small, intimate gathering of a couple of her closest friends and family. Her father, uncle, brother, and sisters sat in the first row of pews. Her sisters looked beautiful in their new dresses, and her father was wearing his best suit. His eyes were troubled, and she could read the look he gave her as clearly as if he'd spoken.

You can still back out, it said. *You can say no.*

She turned back to Mr. Argenton. If he had any apprehension about his bride's answer, she couldn't see it; his face could have been carved from granite.

"I will." She breathed the words more than spoke them, but they were just loud enough for the priest to hear. He nodded and continued the ceremony.

Sophie heard the words but couldn't understand them. Fear coiled through her like a cold, thick snake, ready to strike at her heart. She could only stare at her intended husband, stunned that she was tying her life to that of a stranger.

She'd barely seen him since their engagement. He'd visited her father twice, and she'd greeted him and said goodbye each time. There had been no chance to know him more, though; he'd spent all of his time arranging the wedding. She half wondered if that was his intention in making their marriage day so close—that she would have no time to change her mind.

Though it was impossible to save Sophie from the scandal that would accompany such a brief engagement, it had at least spared her family from having their reduced circumstances known.

The priest offered her a wafer, and Sophie realized she and Mr. Argenton were taking their first communion together. The bread stuck in her dry mouth, but she swallowed it dutifully then sipped the wine.

The ring wrapped her finger, foreign and unnatural. She glanced at Mr. Argenton's eyes and thought she caught a faint glimmer of triumph hidden in their depths. The expression was gone in a flash, though, and he offered her his arm to lead her out of the chapel.

She felt dizzy. As they neared the stairs, her legs buckled, and she had to clutch at his arm to keep herself upright.

"Steady," he murmured, then the doors were opened, and guests showered them in flowers and rice as they emerged into the bright morning sun.

This isn't the right weather at all, Sophie thought dully as she followed Mr. Argenton down the path of petals and toward the waiting carriage. *It should be raining.*

She passed her father and paused to hug him tightly. She wanted to say something—not goodbye, though; she couldn't bring herself to say goodbye—but the words failed her. She thought she saw tears shining in his eyes. Then firm hands helped her up the carriage's stairs.

She leaned forward in her seat to maintain sight of her family for as long as possible. Mr. Argenton climbed inside and sat beside her. Then the door was closed, blocking her view, and the carriage drew forward with a sharp crack from the coachman's whip.

Sophie let the carriage's motion push her into the seat, and she stared wide-eyed at the ceiling, fighting with herself to hold the tears at bay.

"Are you comfortable, my dear?" Mr. Argenton asked.

My dear. The phrase seemed so alien coming from his cool, calm voice that Sophie couldn't immediately reply. She stole a glance at him. He faced directly ahead, but watched her out the corner of his eye. She thought she managed a smile, but she wasn't sure. "Yes, thank you."

She was grateful when he let them lapse into silence.

They were forfeiting the customary celebration meal because Mr. Argenton had said it was urgent that he return to his home before too much time passed, and they needed to start early on the long trip. Sophie's luggage was already loaded onto the carriage. They would pause at an inn ten miles down the road, where they would have a meal and Sophie could change into more comfortable traveling clothes. She had no idea what to expect from their journey beyond that. She'd never been farther north than Abbott, and none of her friends were familiar with Garlow, the closest town.

The trip passed in a blur. The carriage was large, but Mr. Argenton was so lanky that their knees kept bumping. She could feel him watching her. As soon as her throat had cleared enough for her to speak coherently, she said, "It's a beautiful day."

"Yes." A faint smile crept into his voice. "Very fortuitous weather."

She fixed her eyes on her hands, which were clasped in her lap. Her dress was beautiful; it had been made in the latest pattern and layered generously in lace. Her father hadn't said anything, but Sophie was almost certain Mr. Argenton had paid for it.

She wanted to know more about her new home and what sort of life she could expect there, but couldn't find an easy way to bring it up. Instead, she asked, "Is the town a very large one, sir?"

"Joseph."

She glanced up at him, confused, and he raised his eyebrows. "You can call me Joseph."

"Oh." Yes, they were married, but it still felt far too soon to use his Christian name. Far too *intimate*. She didn't want to start their life together on a sour note, though, so she said, "Sophie."

"Sophie," he repeated.

She felt a thrill skip up her spine at the way he enunciated her name. She'd never heard it spoken so carefully before.

"To answer your question, the town is quite small, but pleasant. There are some very good people living there. We don't visit it often, though. Our house is situated nearly twenty miles away."

Twenty miles! That would take hours by coach. Sophie tried not to let alarm show on her face, but she knew she'd failed when Mr. Argenton chuckled. It wasn't a warm or friendly laugh, but something quite bitter. "Yes, my forefathers had exceptionally bad judgment in their choice of location. But my family has lived there for generations."

Sophie tried to come to terms with this news. It would mean isolation to a degree she'd never experienced or even contemplated before. Her father had said few people saw Northwood, but she'd thought that was due to her husband's preference, not circumstance.

Husband. The word hung in her mind. She wondered if she would ever become used to thinking of him as her life partner.

"You're beginning to regret your choice," Mr. Argenton said.

Sophie hurried to fix a smile onto her face. "No, no, not at all! I—that is—it's been so sudden. There's a lot to take in."

He didn't look as though he believed her, but the smallest hint of gentleness crept into his voice. "Your family has been taken care of. I've ensured they will have no concerns for money. You needn't worry for them."

Sophie closed her eyes and exhaled. He'd kept his word, then. Thomas could begin his schooling in the new year as planned. Her sisters would be cared for. And her father could return to the merchant business with no gossip about their misfortune tarnishing his name. "Thank you."

At the same time, something ominous lurked in Mr. Argenton's final phrase. *You needn't worry for them.* It implied that she shouldn't worry about them ever again. By saying "*I will*," she'd separated herself from her birth family forever. It was a horrible idea, and Sophie turned toward the window until she could compose herself.

"You said your aunt, uncle, and cousin stayed with you," she said after a moment. "What are they like?"

Mr. Argenton didn't answer immediately. "I expect they'll like you. I know my cousin, Elise, at the very least, wants company. She'll be glad to have someone a little closer to her own age."

"How old is she?"

"She turned twelve last July."

That made her about the same age as Bella. Sophie was surprised he considered her close to the child's age, but then, at twenty, she supposed she might be nearer to Elise's than to Mr. Argenton's. She didn't like how that made her feel. *Young. Inexperienced.*

They lapsed into silence until the carriage finally pulled to a stop. Sophie peered through the window to see the inn. It was small but looked comfortable. One of the footmen opened the door and helped her out. Mr. Argenton followed. Then he froze, one hand still on the carriage's door, and squeezed his eyes closed. His face had blanched white. Sophie hesitated, uncertain if she should say or do anything, but then he blinked his eyes open and stepped toward her with a tight smile. "Let's go in."

Is he sick? Sophie glanced at his face as he led her through the inn's door. *He's still pale. Does he have an illness he hasn't told me about?*

They were shown to a private room where a meal was already laid out for them. Mr. Argenton waited until Sophie was seated before saying, "I'm afraid I must continue on alone."

She raised her head, surprised. "Sir?"

"Joseph," he corrected. "I have urgent business at Northwood. It's faster if I travel alone, on horseback. You will continue in the carriage. My men will take care of you."

It wasn't a suggestion, but a command. Sophie stared at her plate as she tried to understand what had caused the abrupt change in plans. In some ways, she was relieved by the idea of traveling alone, without the pressure to make small talk with the cool, intense man. It also disturbed her, though. They'd been married less than two hours. It felt too soon to be separated.

"I'll wait for your arrival," Mr. Argenton said. He took her hand, raised it to his lips, and kissed the backs of her fingers. A shock ran through Sophie, and she felt heat rush to her face. But before she could speak, Mr. Argenton turned, left the room, and closed the door behind himself.

Not for the first time, Sophie was left feeling as if she'd escaped a wolf attack. Her heart pounded and her hands trembled as she picked up her cutlery, trying, and failing, to act as though nothing had happened.

She ate quickly, then one of the inn's maids helped her change from her wedding dress into her traveling outfit before she returned downstairs. The footmen, who were waiting by the carriage, helped her inside without a word.

The following three days of travel blurred together into a constant stream of rocking carriages, brief meals, and fitful sleeps. Sophie began to feel the solitude acutely. The footmen never spoke to her, even though she said *good morning* and *thank you* each day. She wondered if they'd been instructed not to interact with her. She started looking forward to the breaks at the inns, where she could have a brief conversation with the maids who brought her food and helped her change.

Every part of the journey had been arranged for her. She was always lodged in the largest room the inn provided and served with far more food than one person could be expected to eat, all of it fresh and expensive. She asked after Mr. Argenton at each stop, and the innkeepers' stories were always the same: he'd stayed overnight but had slept for only a few hours before returning to the road with a fresh horse. The last innkeeper mentioned, with genuine anxiety, that Mr. Argenton had seemed unwell.

That worried Sophie. As she returned to the carriage for the final stretch of the journey, she hoped he wasn't suffering. A small, cruel corner of her mind whispered, *What if he dies?* But she pushed the thought aside with a grimace. *No new bride should ever wish for such a thing.*

It was late afternoon when a voice broke through her thoughts. It was the footman, speaking for the first time since their journey had started. "Welcome to Northwood, Mrs. Argenton."

CHAPTER 5
NORTHWOOD

THEY'D BEEN TRAVELING THROUGH a steadily thickening forest for several hours. Sophie looked out of the window and saw that the trees ahead thinned, giving her a glimpse of the house she was to be mistress of.

Her father had said the building was breathtaking. That was accurate in the same way that describing a peacock as a bird was accurate. Sophie pressed herself to the carriage's side and watched in awe and shock as they descended the hill leading to the building.

It was either three or four stories—she couldn't tell clearly from the distance—and built entirely out of dark stone. Turrets and spires stretched above the black-shingle roof, which was reflecting the last of the late-afternoon sun. There were hundreds of windows. Lights glittered inside a few, but the others, left dark, seemed like dead eyes overseeing the property.

"Sweet mercy," Sophie breathed. She didn't want to think about how many rooms the immense building held.

A little way from the house was a large shadowed lake. The shrubs and small trees growing about the house's sides were not enough to soften the building's stark impression. Sophie thought she caught a glimpse of a vegetable garden behind the house. Not far beyond that, the forest started.

They were unlike any woods Sophie had seen before. The trees were tall and dark. They grew close together, filling their crevices with shadows, and circled the entire estate in a wide arc.

High wrought-iron gates blocked the path, and the carriage pulled to a halt. Sophie expected the footmen to open the gates so they could pass through, but instead, the carriage door was opened, and a hand offered to assist her down.

"We're not driving to the house?" Sophie asked.

"No, Mrs. Argenton. This is as far as the carriage goes."

Sophie looked toward the house again. It was a long walk, and she'd worn one of her nicer dresses to make a good first impression with her new family. But the footman seemed unmovable, so she reluctantly took his hand and climbed down.

As she stepped away from the carriage, she saw the second footman had removed her luggage and piled it neatly beside the gate. She wrung her hands as she stared at them. "Ah... I...I can't carry those myself..."

"No, Mrs. Argenton. They will be collected by the house's staff."

The footmen both climbed back onto the carriage and urged the horses around with a quick flick of the whip.

There was something wrong with the horses, Sophie noticed. Their eyes were wide, exposing the whites, and froth had developed around their mouths where they'd chewed at the bits. They didn't need much encouragement to return to the road, and they pulled the carriage away at what seemed like a much faster pace than they'd approached.

The thunder of hooves faded into the distance, and Sophie found herself really, truly alone for the first time. A cold wind rushed around her, and she pulled her cloak more tightly around her body. The house was to her back, still a ten minutes' walk away, but Sophie couldn't move, despite the quickly failing light. She didn't want to approach the vast building. She didn't want to step over the threshold.

The wood's noises seemed to engulf her. Her ears were filled with owl calls, the mutter of settling birds, and the scraping noise of dead tree branches rubbing together. The longer she stood, the more she became convinced she could hear weedy, whispering voices among the trees.

"Just the leaves," she said to herself. The muttering swelled. Sophie tangled her shaking fingers together and, paralyzed with fear, stared at the litter-strewn path the carriage had taken. She could feel them creeping closer—sightless beings, whispering dead words, dragging their limp forms across the ground, stretching out long fingers to snatch at her dress—

A squeal of metal broke her trance. Sophie gasped and swiveled to face the gates. There were no creatures creeping toward her. Instead, a silhouetted figure had pushed open the gate and stood, one hand on the wrought iron, the other cradling a shotgun, as he regarded her. "You're early, my dear. I'd intended to be here when the carriage arrived."

Sophie exhaled and stepped toward Mr. Argenton. He had his head tilted to one side, and a frown creased his forehead. "You look pale. Is something the matter?"

"No, no, of course not." Sophie shook her head, trying to scatter the fears out of it. *What would he think of me if he knew what I'd been imagining?* Then remembering how the innkeeper had said her husband had been sick, she forgot everything else. "How are you? Are you feeling unwell, sir?"

"Unwell?" His eyebrows rose.

As Sophie moved closer to Mr. Argenton, she searched his face for any gauntness or sick pallor that would suggest chronic illness. But he was no paler than she'd seen him at any other time, and his posture implied easy confidence. He was staring at her with open curiosity, and she blushed. "I—one of the innkeepers said you were unwell—"

"I was in a hurry," he said, offering her his arm. "I had an urgent engagement at Northwood and was probably a little shorter with the staff than I would have otherwise been. But I promise you, I am completely well."

Sophie felt more relieved than she'd expected. She took the offered arm.

As they passed through the gate, she tried to absorb as much of the view as she could in the failing light. The trees, thick and dark, towered above her. She knew it was probably just the way it looked at that time of day, but the entire clearing seemed strangely dim, as though someone had leeched part of its color away, leaving it a sad imitation of what should have been there. Even the lake looked filled with shadows.

Then she remembered that her luggage was still sitting by the gate, and twisted to look back at it. "Ah, my cases—"

"I'll have someone retrieve them presently." Mr. Argenton caught sight of her expression, and the small smile returned. "I can assure you, no one's going to pass by and steal them within the next hour."

They descended the gentle slope leading to the house. The path was uneven and muddy, and Sophie shuddered at how much dirt she knew she was accumulating on her skirts. Mr. Argenton was leading her forward at a brisk pace, though, and she couldn't slow down.

"There are wolves in the woods surrounding our home." Mr. Argenton's abrupt words startled Sophie. "You must never stray far from the house alone. Do you understand?"

A silver glint caught her eye, and she looked toward the open gun hung from the crook of her husband's other arm. "Are they very dangerous?"

"They can be, if you don't know how to deal with them."

No wonder he never has visitors.

More lights were coming on in the house, lighting up dozens of the blank eyes, as twilight progressed toward night.

"I had no idea how large Northwood was," Sophie said. She knew she was clinging to Mr. Argenton's arm more tightly than she should have, but she couldn't stop herself.

"The Argenton family used to be quite extensive. A hundred years ago, the house was full. Now, I'm afraid, it can feel both empty and sadly neglected. We've struggled to find reliable staff."

They reached the base of the hill and crossed the smooth stretch of grass toward the house's entry. Sophie couldn't keep from staring at the grim building. It could have sprung, fully formed, from one of the mythology books that had given her nightmares as a child. Flying buttresses and Gothic balustrades covered its sides, and the arched, church-like windows grew high in the walls. It looked as though it had been constructed by a demented architect; instead of being even and carefully arranged, protrusions and rooms jutted out at strange angles.

Figures were waiting on the steps that led to the front door. Sophie counted more than two dozen of them. She couldn't understand who they were or why they might be there until she drew close enough to see they wore uniforms.

They would be the servants. Did Mr. Argenton summon them to greet me? I suppose I'm their new lady now, aren't I?

The staff bowed as Sophie and Mr. Argenton reached the steps. She smiled at them, but they all kept their eyes fixed on the stone, except for the last one—a young maid, who raised her eyes curiously as Sophie passed.

Mr. Argenton led Sophie through the high arched doorway into the house. Sophie had the impression of stepping through a great maw and into a monster's belly. The foyer was vast and dark, despite the dozen lamps hung about the walls. She could make out a huge stairwell at the back of the room, leading to the second and third floors. The vaulted ceiling extended far above their heads.

Cold chills spread out from her chest, and Sophie didn't realize how fiercely she was squeezing Mr. Argenton's arm until he placed his hand over hers with a soft, "My dear."

She let go immediately and managed to smile, even as she struggled to inhale. The house was beyond daunting; it was thoroughly, crushingly overwhelming. Even the air inside seemed heavier.

Three figures were approaching from the opposite side of the room: a man, nearly as tall as Mr. Argenton but more thickly set, and a woman wearing an expensive, blood-red silk dress. Between them stood a lanky, bleak-faced girl.

The family resemblance was so strong that it was uncanny. All three had pale, long faces, ink-black hair, and dark eyes. The lady, Mr. Argenton's aunt, was the only one whose face held color; her lips had been painted scarlet to match her dress.

"Sophie, I would like you to meet my aunt and uncle, Garrett Argenton and Rose Argenton, and my cousin Elise."

CHAPTER 6
FAVORED VIEW

SMILE! SOPHIE'S MIND SCREAMED at her. She didn't know if her face was forming the right expression. All she knew was that she felt half a minute away from collapsing onto the marble floor.

Rose came toward her, extending both hands to clasp Sophie's. Her blood-red lips parted to expose white teeth, and she pressed forward to kiss both of Sophie's cheeks in an unwanted act of familiarity. The skin that grazed Sophie's face felt cold, and fresh shivers coursed down her back.

"Welcome to Northwood, my dear," Rose said. Her voice was low and throaty, but the words were enunciated perfectly, like her nephew's. Her face was smiling, but something seemed not entirely right about her eyes.

She stepped back, and her husband took her place, clasping Sophie's hand in both of his. His mustache reminded her faintly of her uncle's, but that was where any similarity ended.

Even though he smiled at her, she could tell it was a strange and unnatural expression for his face. He didn't speak and released her hand quickly to return to his place beside his wife.

Elise bowed her head, and Sophie returned the gesture. Unlike her parents, Elise didn't smile. Dark shadows circled her eyes, which seemed too large for her face. Her hair was braided into a tight circle behind her head, and her dress, a modest but expensive cut that was suited to a child who was only a few years away from being considered an adult, clung to her thin frame.

"You chose well," Rose said, turning to Mr. Argenton. "She's quite pretty, Joseph."

It was phrased as a compliment, but coming from Rose, the comment seemed more like a censure. Rose was everything that *pretty* failed to encompass. She was elegant, refined, and the type of glamorous that the city's elite aspired to. Sophie's family had been considered moderately wealthy, but Rose's dress put Sophie's entire wardrobe to shame. Something about the arch of her long neck, how high her cheekbones sat in her face, her straight nose, and the way her silky black hair held its elaborate form perfectly told Sophie that Rose could have been a queen in another life.

Mr. Argenton didn't reply.

"No doubt you'll be tired after your journey," Rose said to Sophie, already turning to leave. "I'll let Joseph show you to your room. I prepared it for you; I do hope you like it. Dinner is at seven precisely. Don't be late."

Sophie found herself taking Mr. Argenton's arm again. She felt as though she were floating through a dream. The foyer's heaviness pressed against her, suffocating her, and a rushing noise filled her ears. Mr. Argenton drew her toward the great staircase at the end of the foyer, and she stumbled on the first step.

"Are you all right, my dear?"

The words were soft, but his voice remained cool. Sophie didn't trust herself to speak, so she nodded and focused on retaining control over her legs for the remaining stairs.

She counted sixty of them. They passed the second floor and stepped off when the stairs opened onto the third. Wide hallways stretched to their left and right, a myriad of doors and more hallways sprouting off them. Mr. Argenton led her right.

"How many rooms are there?" Sophie's voice sounded faint in her own ears.

"Enough" was Mr. Argenton's reply.

The house seemed to be growing darker the farther they pressed into it. The wallpaper, made of rich reds and golds, felt smothered in decadence. Sophie became aware of another set of footsteps behind theirs and glanced over her shoulder. The maid, the young one who'd dared to raise her eyes when Sophie had passed her on the stairs, followed them dutifully.

Mr. Argenton led them deeper into the building, taking so many turns that Sophie began to wonder how she would ever remember the way back. They finally came to the end of a hallway, where a large, dark door waited for them.

"This will be your room," he said, turning the handle. "It has traditionally belonged to the mistress of the property. The view is the most favored in the house."

Sophie felt her breath leave her as the door opened. The room was large and richly furnished. A fire had been started in the hearth, and its golden glow spread across the four-poster bed, the carved bureau, the wardrobe, and the armchairs. The wallpaper, an intricate gold design set on a slate-blue background, was more soothing for her eyes than the hallways, but no more welcoming.

Then she saw the window. It took up a large part of the opposite wall and was so wide that Sophie didn't think she could touch both ends if she stretched her arms. It rose high before curving into multiple arches near the ceiling, and the dark-blue satin curtains had been drawn back to display the outside world. Sophie could barely make out the tips of the trees silhouetted against the last moments of sunset.

Though it was dark out, she knew that her husband hadn't exaggerated. The view would be spectacular.

"How do you like it?" Mr. Argenton asked. "Rose had the furniture and decorations chosen for you."

"It's beautiful. Thank you." Despite the lavishness, Sophie couldn't deny that it had been designed tastefully.

Mr. Argenton stepped to one side, and the maid entered the room after them, curtsying low in deference. Her sandy-brown hair had clearly been fixed up with great care, but strands had slipped out and frizzed around her face.

"This is Marie," Mr. Argenton said. "I hired her from the village to be your lady's maid. She's mute, but she understands instructions well and works hard."

Mute? Sophie glanced at Mr. Argenton, alarmed.

He raised his eyebrows. "Or we can hire a different maid, if you prefer."

"No, no, I'm sure she'll do wonderfully. I'm glad to meet you, Marie." She couldn't say so in front of the girl—especially not when she seemed so eager to please—but Sophie found her husband's choice unsettling. *Why a mute? Are there things he doesn't want her telling me?*

"I'll leave you to change," Mr. Argenton said. "There is still a half hour before dinner. You can summon me a few minutes before seven if you would like help finding your way down."

He bowed and left, and Sophie waited until his brisk steps faded from her hearing before letting her breath out in a rush. She turned back to the room with clear eyes and saw her luggage had been arranged neatly at the foot of her bed. *How did they manage to get it here so quickly? I was only in the foyer for a few minutes.*

Sophie opened one of the cases to find an evening dress and heard Marie inhale at the silks, laces, and satins inside. Sophie pulled out the top dress, a rich-green affair, and shook it out to ensure it hadn't been crushed during the trip. She watched Marie out of the corner of her eye. The maid hovered nearby, hands clasped in front of her apron, eyes shining at the sight of the dresses. "Marie," Sophie began carefully, "have you served as a lady's maid very often before?"

A shake of her head.

"Am I your first?"

A nod.

"And have you been with the Argenton family for long?"

Another shake.

"Well, this will be new to both of us, then." Sophie forced a smile and handed the dress to her assistant.

Mr. Argenton had given her a maid who, on top of being speechless, most likely knew nothing about the house or the family. If he'd wanted to keep secrets, he was being exceptionally thorough about the job.

You're leaping to conclusions. Marie could have been hired with the best of intentions. Perhaps the house's existing staff were too few for one of them to also be my maid. Or maybe Mr. Argenton thought I would be more comfortable with someone equally new to the property.

Either way, Sophie liked the maid quite a lot. She was quick and seemed eager to please, and her brown hair and blue eyes were strikingly out of place in the dark building...which mimicked exactly how Sophie felt.

Once the dress was in place, Marie stepped back and clapped her hands, a wide smile dimpling her cheeks. Sophie appreciated the encouragement and returned the smile. "I think I'd like to be alone for a few minutes before dinner, please. Thank you, Marie."

Marie curtsied and left the room, and Sophie sank down onto the edge of her bed. The abrupt silence threatened to drown her in its weight.

CHAPTER 7
THE RED DOOR

SOPHIE DIDN'T MOVE FOR several long minutes, but focused on her hands, which were still shaking. *Mistress of Northwood.* The title should have belonged to Rose, who must have handled the task with great finesse before Sophie arrived.

Why did he marry me? Could he really imagine me fitting in here? Caring for Northwood as he cares for it?

Sophie stood and paced the length of her room. The thick carpet sank under her feet. The fire, which had been built up well, sent shadows skittering over the walls. Sophie found herself standing before the window and gazing into the pitch-black outside. Even from a distance, she could hear the woods; the trees groaned as the wind stretched them, moving the gigantic black trunks and scraping their boughs together.

Sophie shuddered and turned away. A door on the other side of her bed caught her attention, and she went to it. It opened into a second bedroom. A large bed stood against the opposite wall, and the bureau held shaving equipment and combs. *Mr. Argenton's.*

The room was impeccably clean. Its fire hadn't yet been lit, and the air felt cold, almost frosty. Not wanting to disturb her husband's domain, Sophie retreated, closing the door tightly behind herself. There was no lock.

She turned toward her fireplace's mantel, where a clock ticked steadily toward seven. There were still ten minutes until dinner, but Sophie decided she would rather be early than late on her first night. She checked her hair in the mirror—it looked even more bizarre than normal when contrasted with the dark walls—then took up one of the lamps and left her room, closing the door behind herself.

Down the hallway until it splits, then…left, I think?

She'd been so anxious on her arrival that she couldn't remember the path, but she followed the main passageways, hoping one would eventually lead her to the staircase. The house's halls were disorienting and didn't seem to follow any order. She found herself at the top of the servant's stairwell at one point and had to backtrack.

Her anxiety began to rise, and Sophie increased her pace. The house truly felt like a maze. The wallpaper, all reds and golds, disoriented her. *Didn't I already pass that door? What wing am I in?*

Sophie turned down what seemed to be a main passageway and found herself confronted by a strange sight. The hallway, although long, had no doors leading off it. Unlike the rest of the house, the wallpaper was black and gold. At the end of the hallway was a single door, wide enough for two people to walk through and nearly reaching the ceiling. It had been painted a violent red.

What a bizarre door. What's beyond it?

Sophie followed the stark hallway, her curiosity driving the dinner appointment from her mind. She thought she could hear some sort of noise—a rustling, almost like the sounds the trees had made, with whispers contained inside. They seemed to be calling to her, urging her forward. The door's black handle glinted in the dim candlelight, and Sophie reached for it, mesmerized.

"That's the wrong way," a voice said, and Sophie jumped so badly that her lamp spluttered. She turned and saw Elise standing at the end of the hallway. The girl's deep-set eyes watched her impassively. "Dinner will begin in a moment. Mother will be angry if you're late."

"Oh, yes, of course." Sophie pressed a hand to her thundering heart. "I'm sorry. I was lost."

"Follow me."

The girl's tone was just as emotionless as Mr. Argenton's. She turned and disappeared without waiting to see if her companion was following. Sophie had to jog to catch up.

Elise's brisk walk and unwavering stare didn't invite conversation, but Sophie still felt as though she should say something. "Do you dine with us?"

"No."

"Oh. Of course. You probably eat with your governess."

"I don't have one." Elise took a sharp turn, and Sophie had to jog again to catch up. "I used to, but she died. Father hasn't been able to find a replacement."

Sophie had no idea what to say to that, but Elise stopped, and Sophie saw they were at the top of the grand staircase.

"Go to the ground floor and through the door to your left," Elise said, already turning to retrace her steps. "There's only one minute until seven."

Sophie swallowed, picked up her skirts, and hurried down the stairs. As she reached the foyer, a grandfather clock somewhere deeper in the house chimed. Sophie turned left, crossed the white-tile expanse, and pushed through the double doors. She found herself in the dining room, where Mr. Argenton was waiting, along with Rose and Garret Argenton.

"Right on time," Rose said as the clock fell silent. She examined Sophie with a curious smile, and her thin eyebrows rose.

Sophie had thought she'd chosen her outfit well. It was stately and dignified—the exact impression she wanted to give for her first evening at Northwood. However, compared to Rose's, it seemed sad and limp.

A little behind Rose, Mr. Argenton also watched her, and his faint smile gave Sophie hope that his impression was more positive than his aunt's. He beckoned her toward the table and indicated the seat at the head. He took his own place opposite her, and the four of them sat.

Sophie tried to take in the room without seeming as though she were examining it. Like everything else in Northwood, it was lavish, elegant, and cloaked in shadows. The table was large enough for an extra half a dozen guests, and the plates were fine china. Sophie felt dwarfed by the size of the room. She wished they could have moved to a smaller, more intimate setting.

The footmen entered through a door behind Sophie and began serving the soup entrée. Sophie thought it might be mushroom. After a moment, Rose interrupted the clink of metal on china.

"I trust you had a good journey, my dear."

My dear. It sounded strange when Mr. Argenton said it, but that was by far preferable to the slivers of condescension lacing his aunt's voice.

Sophie managed a smile. "Yes, thank you."

"I hope the footmen were polite. I would have preferred to send some of our own, but they couldn't be spared. It's always concerning to hire outsiders. One never knows if they'll do their jobs adequately."

If you want to know that they kept silent as instructed, I can assure you they did. "They were very polite."

"That's good to hear." Although Rose was smiling, it didn't extend to her eyes. Sophie realized that was what had bothered her in the foyer. They were dead eyes—clever, yes, and proud, but also soulless.

The footmen removed the soup bowls and brought in herb-roasted duck and green vegetables. The food had been prepared beautifully, and Sophie, who hadn't eaten since a brief stop at the inn shortly after noon, was ravenous. "This looks delicious."

Mr. Argenton gave her a small nod of thanks. "It all comes

from the estate. Wild duck, fish from the lake, vegetables and fruit from our garden. With such a distance separating us from the town, we must be as self-reliant as possible."

"It's a beautiful spread."

"A celebration dinner," Rose said, her red lips parting in the same dead smile. "To welcome our new bride."

Garrett Argenton, who hadn't said a word all evening, glanced toward Mr. Argenton. Sophie saw her husband shake his head in answer, and both gentlemen returned to their meals.

"I'm sure you'll wish to rest tonight, my dear," Rose continued, "but perhaps in the morning, I can show you about the house, so you can learn what tasks must be done each day to keep Northwood running smoothly. I'm sure you're eager to apply your own touch to the estate."

"I—" It was the sort of question that her mother's gentle tact would have easily saved, but Sophie only managed to splutter, "I'm sure there's not much to change. It's been in your family for so long—"

The corners of Rose's mouth turned down, but she waved away the fumbled objections. "No, my dear, you're in charge now. You must make it *your* house."

I'm not sure that's possible. Sophie bowed her head. The duck, juicy and perfectly seasoned, seemed far less appetizing than it had before.

Of course Rose won't want the house changed. Anything I alter will be seen as a censure of her choices. Her question was a test, and I failed.

The silence drew on, and Sophie desperately searched for a

comment to soothe her aunt. "My room is beautiful. You said you decorated it, didn't you?"

"Hmm. I'm pleased you like it, my dear."

"And I'm afraid I became a little lost on the way to dinner, but everything I saw of the house was perfect. You have impeccable taste."

Rose's lips curled into a smile, and Sophie felt a rush of relief. She didn't think she'd completely saved the situation, but at least Rose's vanity had been pacified.

"Did you find your way to the west wing? My favorite sitting room is there. I answer my letters in it in the mornings."

"I don't think I saw it, no." Eager to stay on a safe subject, Sophie added, "I found a very curious red door, though."

A clatter made her start. Mr. Argenton had dropped his fork. He half rose from his seat, his lips fixed into a thin line, as something dangerous glittered in his dark eyes.

Oh no, oh no, no, no. He's angry. I did something wrong. What? Sophie opened her mouth to apologize, but she had no idea what to say. Her mind raced as the panic rose inside her.

"Don't go through that door, my dear," Mr. Argenton said. His voice was no longer cool; it was ice-cold. "You shouldn't have been in that part of the house."

"I'm sorry." The words escaped as a whisper, and Sophie wasn't sure he'd heard. The fragile civility of the dinner table was dissolving, and she desperately tried to save it. "I-I didn't know. I'm so sorry—"

Rose and Garrett Argenton had placed their cutlery on their

plates. Garrett's face was blank, but Rose's mouth held a faint hint of amusement. For the first time, Sophie thought she saw a spark of life in the older woman's eyes.

"This is her home now," Rose said, her words laced with barely hidden delight. "I'm not sure you can forbid her from exploring it, dear nephew."

"She's *my* wife." Mr. Argenton's voice was low and dangerous.

Sophie clasped her hands in her lap and fixed her eyes on her half-empty plate. Through the fear, she fought to understand his meaning. *"She's my wife, and she'll follow my orders,"* or *"She's my wife, and I'll decide how much of the house she sees"*?

And what was wrong with the red door?

Rose and Mr. Argenton stared at each other for several long moments. Finally, Rose waved her hand with a displeased huff and picked up her fork. "Very well, but it can't continue for long."

What can't?

Sophie barely dared to look at Mr. Argenton. His eyes had fixed on her again, and the scrutiny sent panicky prickles across her skin.

"Sophie." His voice was softer than before but held a steely edge of authority. "There are parts of this house that none of us go into. That door is one of them. If you wish to please me, you will promise me not to open it."

Anything. Please just don't be angry. "Yes, I promise."

Mr. Argenton continued to watch her for a moment then moved back into his seat and picked up his fork. The room was silent. Desperate to maintain control of herself and stop the frightened tears that pricked at her eyes, Sophie tried to eat. Her throat was tight, and she couldn't swallow, so she busied herself with cutting her meat into smaller pieces and bumping the vegetables across the plate, hoping she wouldn't look as agitated as she felt. When she finally dared to glance at Mr. Argenton again, she found he'd pushed his plate to one side and was watching her above his laced fingers. He was frowning.

It was a relief when the dinner plates were exchanged for dessert, and at last, the puddings and pies, barely touched by any of them, were also taken away.

Rose stood first. "Would you care to join me for some tea, my dear?"

Speak clearly. Don't let them see you're upset. "Thank you, but I—I'm afraid I am quite tired."

"Of course, you'll want an early bed. Shall I show you the way?"

"I'll show her," Mr. Argenton said, rounding the table. The terse note was back in his voice.

Rose watched him through half-lidded eyes for a moment, then inclined her head and left the room.

Sophie stared at the arm offered to her. Rejecting it would have been an insult, but taking it somehow seemed risky. She desperately wished she knew the way to her room and could beg to be left alone.

Mr. Argenton's gaze was steady. She felt as though he could see into her mind and read the panic there. When he spoke, his voice was gentle. "Sophie."

She didn't want the dangerous tone to return. She looped her arm through his and resolutely focused her eyes on the floor so that he wouldn't see inside them again.

Mr. Argenton led her back to the staircase. They climbed to the third floor in silence, turned right, and began weaving through the passageways. After a few turns, Mr. Argenton drew them to a halt.

Is he still angry? Should I say something?

Mr. Argenton's free hand covered Sophie's, and he sighed. It was a deep, regretful sound. When he spoke, his voice was softer than she'd ever heard it. "You're shaking. Was I really that brutish?"

Don't let him think you're weak. "No, no, of course not."

"Yes, I was." Mr. Argenton removed her arm from his, raised her hand to his mouth, and pressed his lips to her knuckles. His breath felt warm on her skin, and Sophie finally raised her eyes to look at him.

The stony expression was gone. In its place, he looked sad—deeply, as though he would have given a lot to take back his words.

He lowered her hand but didn't release it. "Sophie, I'm sorry for how I spoke over dinner. I was only concerned for you. You had no way of knowing, but that part of the house is crumbling and unstable. If you visit it, you're in very great danger of falling through the floor or being crushed. The door is painted red to warn the staff away. You mustn't ever enter it."

"I won't."

He ran his thumb across the backs of her fingers. The gesture was soft and strangely comforting. Sophie found herself lost in his eyes. *So dark, they could be black.*

He took a half step nearer, closing the distance between them. There was a hint of something more in his gaze. Something heated. He raised his hand to her cheek and caressed her skin, pushing the curls back. His fingers were firm but careful, and Sophie, against her better judgment, leaned into his touch. *That feels...nice.*

A door slammed.

Startled, Sophie stepped back. Mr. Argenton blinked at her, then sighed and offered his arm again. "I won't keep you up any longer," he said, the even, cool note back in his voice. "You must be tired."

Sophie hesitated, glancing between her husband and the direction of the noise that had startled her, then took his arm. He led her at a slower, calmer pace until they stopped at her door.

"Would you like anything tonight? Some tea?"

"Thank you, I'm fine."

"I'll send your maid to help you change."

Sophie wanted nothing more than to be alone. She gave a small bow. "Don't disturb her. I'll be very comfortable myself. Thank you."

He raised her hand to his lips and kissed it before turning to disappear into the hallway's shadows.

CHAPTER 8
ROSE

SOPHIE EXHALED AND PRESSED her back to the closed door. The evening's events swirled through her mind like a toxic soup. *The red door. Rose's smirks. And Mr. Argenton—*

"Stop it." Sophie pressed her hands over her eyes and focused on her breathing. *Inhale, exhale. Slow and even. Regain control. Don't fall apart now.*

As her shaking settled and her mind calmed, Sophie tried to examine that night's events as rationally as she could. Mr. Argenton had explained why he'd forbidden her from opening the red door, but Sophie couldn't believe him entirely. His reaction at the dinner table had been too immediate and harsh. If it had been as simple as a set of dilapidated rooms, why hadn't he just told her, instead of demanding a promise to stay away?

She would keep her word, of course. No matter how much her curiosity bit at her, not angering Mr. Argenton was more important. She could bear anything as long as her company was agreeable.

And Mr. Argenton had been *very* agreeable when he'd stopped to speak with her in the hallway.

I'd never have expected he could be that gentle...that warm...

Color rose across Sophie's cheeks as she remembered the sensation of his fingers on her skin. She couldn't believe how *right* it had felt. For the first time since her engagement, her future didn't seem entirely bleak. *Maybe we can learn to like each other. I don't need love...and I don't dare even hope for it...but I do want him to like me.*

An owl hooted outside. The moon had risen over the treetops and bathed the property in its cool blue light. Sophie crossed to the window and gasped as movement caught her attention.

A doe grazed on the lawn. Moonlight glittered off its form as it raised its graceful head to check for danger, then bent again to tear up more grass. Sophie, who hadn't seen anything more exciting than horses since her family had moved to the city, held her breath as she watched. It seemed magical. The deer moved slowly as it ate, its lanky legs carrying it closer to the building until it disappeared from view.

Sophie reluctantly looked away from the window. The hour was growing late, and she still needed to change. That was when she realized her cases no longer stood at the foot of her bed.

Did the staff unpack them?

She opened her wardrobe and took a reflexive step back. Her dresses and bonnets were nowhere to be seen. Instead, the hangers were filled with dark lace and silk dresses. They were far more elegant than anything Sophie owned, and they reminded her of Rose's dresses. Sophie pulled one out and stared at it, confused.

This is *my room, isn't it?*

"Do you like them, my dear?"

Sophie swiveled so quickly that her back bumped the wardrobe. She wanted to cry out, but her throat had constricted too much to make a noise.

Rose glided through the open doorway, a cold smirk growing across her red lips. "I hope you don't mind, but I had your wardrobe replaced during dinner. Your old dresses would all do very well for the city, I'm sure, but they don't become you now that you're in Northwood."

Sophie felt as though she might collapse from shock. She clutched at the wardrobe's door to keep her feet. "How—how—"

"Don't worry; they will all fit. I had them made to the same measurements as your wedding dress." Rose offered a wolfish grin. "You haven't put on weight since last week, have you?"

Sophie wanted to demand her old dresses back and reject the unwanted gifts, but part of her knew spurning her aunt's will would be a grave mistake. "My old clothes, where—"

"Incinerated." Rose was gliding closer, her voice a dangerous purr. "These will suit you much better. And Joseph will enjoy them. I know what he likes. Though it doesn't look like you need any help catching his eye, do you?"

Sophie's mind raced. "You—was that you slamming the door?"

"You're a clever girl, aren't you? Well, then, I'm sure you'll understand my meaning now—don't grow too close to my nephew." Rose pinched Sophie's jaw in her red-tipped fingers and tilted her head up so that their gazes met. "Don't let him into your heart. For both of your sakes."

Sophie's mouth was too dry for her to reply. She tried to shrink back, but Rose's grip was like a vice. They stood, locked in silence, Sophie's heartbeat a loud staccato rhythm in her ear. Then Rose leaned an inch closer, pushing farther into Sophie's personal space. "Wear this white one tomorrow," she murmured, running her free hand across a floating organza dress. "Coupled with your hair, you'll look like an angel. Good night, my dear."

Rose released Sophie's chin then strode out of the room, leaving Sophie to collapse to the ground and fight back her hysteria.

The meeting had thoroughly doused any hope that had grown over that evening. She couldn't live in Northwood. Couldn't share her table with the calculating, cutting Rose. Couldn't let herself stay long enough to see what the members of the Argenton family were capable of if they were pushed too far.

What else can you do, though? You can't return to the city or to your father. And if you run away, you have no money and no recommendations to secure you any sort of job. You'd be reduced to a beggar...or a street worker. And even if you somehow, miraculously found a way to survive on your own, you couldn't stay hidden for long. If Mr. Argenton wanted to find you, he would uncover you in an instant.

Tears finally slipped out. Sophie tried to fight them, but once they'd started, there was no chance of stopping the flow. She staggered to her feet and went to the room's door, which she closed and bolted. Then she began tugging off her dress. She didn't bother taking her usual care with it; she was certain Rose would have it incinerated the following day.

The tears evolved into sobs as Sophie pulled on the new

nightdress. It was silky, elegant, and well made—exactly the sort of nightdress Rose would wear. Sophie hated it. She would have almost preferred to sleep naked.

But she already knew any sort of rebellion would be crushed. She had no doubts that Rose could be ruthless when she wanted something. *And what she wants is for me to keep my distance from Mr. Argenton. Why?*

The immediate burn of fear and disappointment had spent itself. Sophie wiped at the tear tracks staining her cheeks and sat on the edge of the bed to watch the window.

The deer was still grazing on the lawn. Some of the ache in her chest ebbed as she watched the peaceful creature eat.

You don't feel it, do you? she silently asked the doe. *This house is nothing but a dark block of bricks to you. You can't feel the tremendous, crushing weight of its secrets.*

A door nearby opened and closed, and Sophie heard the sounds of water being poured. Mr. Argenton was going to bed. Sophie felt a flush of anxiety and straightened her back, suddenly aware of how much skin the new nightdress showed.

She stared at the door that connected their rooms—*the door with no locks*—and listened to her husband wash and change. At last, there was the sizzle of his lamp being extinguished, then a rustle as he got into bed. Sophie stayed up for nearly twenty more minutes, waiting, but the door remained closed.

She couldn't tell if she felt more relieved or disappointed.

CHAPTER 9
NIGHT'S MELODY

SOPHIE STARTED AWAKE. MOONLIGHT dampened by thin clouds slipped through the windows to create patterns across her bed. The forest's symphony echoed around her as she sat up and pushed her hair away from her face. The fire had died, save for a cluster of weak, glowing coals huddled in the gray soot.

A note floated to her. It was low, hung in the air for a long time, and seemed to come from a piano deep in the house. As Sophie held her breath, a second note was played, then a third, blending into something unpleasant. They were held for far too long, until they made Sophie squeeze her eyes closed, then were abruptly released.

It must be after two in the morning. Why is the piano being played now?

The notes resumed, this time in a melody. Sophie drew a sharp breath. The tune was both exquisite and ghastly. The notes jarred together, discordant, but somehow managing to create a captivating, aggressive tune.

Sophie slipped out of bed and wrapped her arms around her torso. The room had become cold without the fire, and she shivered. She moved to the door and nudged it open, letting the melody reach her more clearly.

It seemed to be coming from all around her at once. The deep notes from her left; the high ones from her right, and the rest hovering above her head and below her feet. It was a song that matched the house perfectly. Disharmonic, but blended into a unified whole. Deep and dark and mysterious. *Dangerous.*

The music swelled into frenzy, its volume increasing until Sophie clutched her hands over her ears in an attempt to block it out. Then with a final, angry clash of keys, it fell silent. Sophie, shivering, slowly lowered her hands. If Mr. Argenton had heard the song, he didn't stir from his room.

Something tickled her right wrist, and Sophie touched it. It was a liquid, strange and tacky, that clung to her skin. With a final glance down the hallway, Sophie returned to her room and bolted the door behind herself. She knelt by the low-burning embers to see what had dripped on her.

It was hard to tell in the dim light, but she thought the liquid might be red. *It's not blood. Don't think that.*

Sophie licked at her dry lips then hurried to her bureau, where she poured fresh water from the jug into the basin and scrubbed the drop from her wrist.

She sat on the stool for a long time, glancing from the dark window to the barely visible doorway. She doubted she would be able to sleep. Instead, she pulled her dressing gown—*no, Rose's gown*—from the wardrobe, wrapped it tightly around herself, and lit a candle in the embers. She then sat at her desk, placed a clean sheet of paper on the table, uncorked the inkwell, and dipped her pen into the swirling black pot.

The light was too poor to see well, so Sophie bent low over the paper as she began writing in a carefully controlled script.

Dear Father…

CHAPTER 10
THE DOE

WHEN SOPHIE STIRRED THE next morning, the sun's light was so dim that she thought it must still be night. She turned toward the window and saw thick, dark clouds had gathered over the sky.

The air was ice-cold, and Sophie regretted not salvaging the fire when she'd woken the night before. She wrapped the dressing gown around herself as she approached the huge window.

It was her first proper look at the view. The grass, dull and gray, stretched away from the house, sloping gradually downward until it hit the edge of the clearing. The trees then grew upward in a stiff wall that reminded Sophie of a prison fence. One corner of the lake was visible to her right. She thought she saw something stirring in it. Mr. Argenton had said they ate fish from the property. *The lake must be stocked.*

Sophie looked downward and clasped a hand over her mouth.

The doe lay on the ground below her window. Its beautiful

eye stared up at her, blank in death, a dribble of blood flowing from its corner to stain the fur. A cluster of black shapes on the corpse shifted, and Sophie realized they were crows—nearly a dozen of them—gathered around their meal.

The doe had been so serene the night before. To see its lifeless form crumpled on the grass, becoming prey to the nature it had once cohabitated with, was horrific. Sophie turned away from the window and pressed her palms to her eyes.

Death is natural. It's nothing to cry over.

A clock somewhere in the house chimed. Sophie counted the deep, somber notes. *Eight...nine...ten. Did I really sleep so late?* That wouldn't make a good impression among the staff. Sophie crossed to the bell beside her bed and tugged it to summon Marie.

The maid arrived in less than a minute. Sophie thought she must have run the distance, based on the way she was panting. It felt good to have some cheerful company, and Sophie beamed at her maid's round, eager face. "Ready, Marie?"

A nod. Sophie opened her wardrobe and flicked through its contents. She hesitated a second then reluctantly chose the white dress Rose had told her to wear. "Mrs. Argenton—Rose—thought I might like some new dresses," Sophie explained when she felt Marie's eyes on the wardrobe. "How about this one?"

After another nod, Marie took the dress with a wide smile.

As she changed, Sophie found her thoughts returning to the haunting music she'd heard the night before. Marie would live in a very different part of the house—probably the fourth floor—and might have heard things Sophie couldn't have. "Marie, were you woken by the piano last night?"

Marie froze halfway through lacing Sophie into the dress. Her mouth opened a fraction then closed, and she shook her head.

Sophie, curious, watched her maid in the mirror and chose her next words carefully. "I heard music in the early hours of the morning. But Mr. Argenton told me none of his family played. Do you think one of the staff might have a musical inclination, Marie?"

Marie shook her head, this time without any hesitation.

"I see. Do you have any idea who it was, then?"

Shaking her head, Marie kept her eyes fixed on the laces, and Sophie could feel her fingers shaking.

She lowered her voice to a gentle murmur. "Marie, did someone tell you not to talk to me about the piano?"

Marie looked up, startled, and met Sophie's gaze. She neither nodded nor shook her head, but her eyes were wide and frightened.

Sophie knew she'd hit on the truth. "It's all right, Marie, you don't have to answer."

There was so much more that Sophie wanted to know, but she knew Marie wasn't the person to ask. She was too new to the estate to know much about it, and what she did know, she was reluctant to share. Even though Marie was Sophie's maid, her employment relied on Mr. Argenton and Rose, and she was bound by their instructions.

With the dressing complete, Marie helped Sophie with her

hair. As she bundled the fine, light strands into a sweet design, Marie mimed a heart shape on her breast. *I love your hair.*

Sophie felt a smile, a genuine one, spread over her face. "Thank you," she whispered back.

A second maid interrupted just as Marie finished pinning Sophie's hair, and left a tray of tea and cookies. Sophie asked Marie if she would like to stay and have breakfast with her, but her maid gestured that she was needed elsewhere in the house. Sophie was left alone with her thoughts as she drank the steaming tea.

She would need to find someone to deliver the letter she'd written to her father the night before. She'd been careful about what she'd said, and Sophie thought she'd managed to avoid any hints of unhappiness or implications that Northwood was anything except a grand home. Worrying her father wouldn't help anyone.

She missed her family painfully. The homesickness squeezed at her insides, making her heart hurt and her stomach churn. She didn't know how frequently mail was delivered at Northwood, but she hoped she would have a reply letter soon. Any news from home, even mundane news, would be like a feast for a starving man.

She drank the tea but couldn't stomach the cookie, and uncertain about what to do with the tray, she left it outside her door.

The house's oppressive darkness pressed on her as she stood in the doorway with the letter clutched in her hands. Lamps had been lit along the hallways, but long stretches of shadows gathered between them. Sophie straightened her shoulders, clasped her hands over the sealed letter so tightly that they began to ache, and started into the maze of passageways.

Footsteps approached, then a maid, carrying a fresh pail of wood to refill one of the fireplaces, rounded a corner ahead.

Relief spread through Sophie's chest, and she hurried to catch up. "Good morning!"

The maid turned at the sound of Sophie's voice and gave a slight curtsy. Sophie came to a halt in front of her and waited for a return of the greeting, but didn't receive a reply.

She's not mute, too, is she? What if Mr. Argenton only employs servants who can't speak?

The thought chilled her, and Sophie hurried on before it could become embedded. "I'm still learning my way through the house. Could you direct me to the stairs, please?"

"That way." One pale hand rose to point to the pathway the maid had just come from.

"Oh, thank you so much."

Again, there was no reply. Sophie, trying not to look as uncertain as she felt, took the passageway. She could feel the maid's eyes following her.

The hallway ended on a new, wider pathway, and Sophie hesitated. The maid hadn't given any further directions. She turned right, but it only led into a system of offshoots and doors. Sophie was trying to backtrack when she heard a faint humming noise.

It almost sounds like the song that was played last night.

Sophie let her ears guide her closer to the eerie tune, until she pushed through a door and found herself in a large, well-furnished sitting room. Rose was behind the desk, a stack of open letters laid out before her, and her quill hovered over a fresh sheet of paper. She fell silent as Sophie entered.

"I'm sorry. I didn't mean to disturb you," Sophie said as the fluttery, anxious feeling returned to her chest.

Rose looked very different by day. The intensity that had haunted her eyes when she'd confronted Sophie had receded back to the dead glaze. Sophie tried to duck out of the room quickly, but Rose beckoned her closer. "You've found my favorite sitting room, my dear."

"Oh, this is the west wing? I didn't know—I just followed your humming. Were you playing the piano last night?"

Rose tilted her head to one side, a curious half smile showing her white teeth. "What an odd thing to ask. I don't play, and we keep the piano locked when we don't have company."

Her tone brought a flush of embarrassment to Sophie's cheeks. "Oh, I thought—"

"Perhaps it was a dream, my dear. I suppose it's to be expected that you're a little out of sorts after such a long trip." Rose's eyes fell to the letter Sophie clutched. "You have something to post. Lovely. Would you like me to take care of it for you? I was just finishing my own replies for this morning."

"Thank you." Sophie hesitated only a second before handing the precious letter to Rose. The older woman placed it on top of a bundle of her own correspondence.

"The mail doesn't come to Northwood very often, but I'll be sure to give you the reply as soon as it arrives." Rose placed her pen into the inkwell and stood. "Now, I believe I promised to show you about the house this morning. Shall we?"

Sophie obediently followed Rose from the room. She wanted to ask where Mr. Argenton was, but Rose's command—*don't let him get too close*—still echoed in her ears. She didn't want to say anything that might anger her aunt, especially now that civilities seemed to have been restored.

Rose led her to the stairs and down to the ground floor. She turned right and pushed through a heavy door that opened into the kitchens. The cook and her assistants fell silent as Rose and Sophie entered the room. Every set of eyes dropped to the floor as their tasks—even a pot of sauce that was beginning to boil over—were ignored. Rose watched them, a smirk hovering about her mouth, then said, "Continue."

As one, the staff turned back to their jobs, carefully avoiding any eye contact.

They're terrified of her, Sophie realized, and her stomach churned. *What has she done to them?*

"As mistress of Northwood, you will be responsible for giving instructions for our meals each day," Mrs. Argenton said. "Of course, any fresh food you order, whether meat or vegetable, must come from the estate. Different foods have different seasons. To arrange a harmonic meal, you must keep in mind which foods are currently available. You wouldn't want to order the trout without there being any chervil to make the sauce, would you?"

Sophie shook her head. The anxiety had returned to bite at her, reminding her that any and every mistake would be judged harshly.

Rose's smile grew. "Of course, having lived on the estate for all of my life, I'm very familiar with which foods are in season at any time. That's the only way I've been able to ensure the dinner table is always pleasant." She tilted her head to one side. "Do you think you're capable of the same task?"

Sophie's mouth felt too dry to allow her to answer properly. The bustle of the kitchen wasn't helping; scullery maids wove about the room while the cook whispered instructions. Pots boiled, knives scraped against chopping boards, and the smell of cloves and garlic felt thick about Sophie's head.

Rose interpreted the silence as she chose. "Or, if you prefer, I could maintain control of the meal arrangements for the time being. Only until you're more familiar with our systems, of course."

"I'd be very grateful," Sophie managed.

Rose squeezed her arm and led her out of the room with a self-satisfied smile.

Just like that, she's secured control of the kitchens. Well, that suits me fine. Nobody likes change; anything I alter about Northwood, even unintentionally, is certain to upset Rose and probably disturb Mr. Argenton, too.

"I'll show you how to manage the maids and the house's maintenance," Rose said as they returned to the vast foyer. Sophie thought she could guess where this was going to lead, and she wasn't surprised when Rose added, "It's quite a tricky job. Northwood is an old and peculiar house, with many quirks that need to be cared for."

This time, Sophie knew what her aunt wanted to hear. "It sounds as though it would be very easy to make a mistake if I don't know the house well."

"*Very* easy."

"Perhaps you would be considerate enough to assist me with the task?"

She'd said the magic words. Rose's mouth opened into a wide smile, and her dead eyes sparkled. "Certainly, my dear. I can arrange everything, if you like, until you feel confident taking over."

"That would be wonderful."

"Then we have an accord." Rose squeezed Sophie's arm a second time and returned to the stairs to finish her letters.

Sophie felt part of the anxiety ease away. Rose would remain as mistress of Northwood in all but name; in return, Sophie hoped she'd bought at least a little goodwill.

CHAPTER 11
STORM

SOPHIE HOVERED IN THE foyer. Without the house to manage, she didn't know what to do with her morning. She went to the front door and pushed it open a crack to see if she could explore the grounds, but the dark clouds had thickened. The rain would start soon; she would have to wait for the storm to clear.

She turned back to the stairwell, wishing she could return to her room and its beautiful solitude, but the maids would need to clean it, and she didn't want to inconvenience them by making them wait. Besides, she still didn't know her way.

Maybe I can find a sitting room like Rose's and write letters. Except she had no one to write to besides her family, and she was already sending them a letter that day.

A door slammed to her right, and Sophie heard a voice echo through the rooms. "Have you seen Mrs. Argenton? *No*—Sophie—my wife. Where is she?"

The voice was harsh, and Sophie cringed backward. The door's cold wood pressed into her shoulders, and she wished she could melt through it and disappear into the outside world before Mr. Argenton found her.

He's angry again. What have I done this time?

The dining room door burst open. Mr. Argenton stood in the entrance, his dark hair ruffled and his eyes wild. He caught sight of Sophie and, to her surprise, exhaled. The tension left his shoulders, and he slumped for a second before collecting himself. When he crossed the foyer toward her, his face held none of the anger she'd feared. Instead, he looked relieved.

"There you are." He took her hand in his. It was almost a reflexive motion, as though he wasn't fully conscious of doing it, and he rubbed at her palm with his thumb. "I've been looking for you all through the house."

"Rose was showing me the kitchens," Sophie managed. She didn't want to admit to herself how good his hand felt. It was firm and comforting. Heat crept across her cheeks. "Is everything all right, Mr. Argenton?"

A faint smile tugged at his mouth. "You're determined not to use my name, aren't you? And yes. I'm fine now."

"Oh." Sophie met his eyes and felt her foolish, happy smile grow. Then thunder cracked outside, and she shuddered.

"Are you afraid of storms, my dear?" Mr. Argenton brushed a stray curl behind her ear. Some type of emotion—Sophie wasn't sure what—flickered in his eyes.

Don't let him get too close.

Sophie took a half step backward. Mr. Argenton let her move away, though he frowned as he dropped her hand. Sophie searched for something to say and stumbled on, "A doe died outside my room last night."

"Ah, you saw it." The coolness had returned to his voice.

Sophie felt a pang of regret.

"I found it while visiting the gardens this morning. I'm sorry it had to expire so near to your room. I'll have my men move it to the forest."

Sophie nodded. Another peal of thunder, closer this time, seemed to shake the house.

"I'm going hunting," Mr. Argenton continued. "I shouldn't be away too long. Will you be able to amuse yourself in the meantime?"

Sophie turned toward the door in alarm. "Now—but it's about to rain!"

The faint, fluttering smile returned. "I expect it to hold for another few hours. And besides, rain won't hurt me."

"You could catch a cold," Sophie rebuffed.

Mr. Argenton's smile faded. "I never do. Perhaps you would like to spend some time with Elise while I'm out. She would love to know you better."

That caught Sophie off guard. She would have preferred to be alone, but knew she should be spending time becoming familiar with her new family. "I—yes—I'd be delighted."

"She will be in the library. The butler can show you the way."

As he spoke, Mr. Argenton turned to someone behind Sophie,

and she swiveled with a start. A butler, his face deeply creased, stood behind them, holding a shotgun. Mr. Argenton took the rifle, and the butler gave a low bow. "If you will follow me, Mrs. Argenton."

Sophie felt as though she should argue against Mr. Argenton leaving the house. The clouds were so thick and dark that it was pure fantasy to imagine the rain would hold off for more than ten minutes, but Mr. Argenton had already pushed open the door and was disappearing down the steps. Sophie waited until the closing doors blocked him from view, then she reluctantly turned to the butler, who bowed again and began to lead her toward the staircase.

CHAPTER 12
WHISPERS

THE BUTLER'S SHOES MADE quiet clicking noises on the wooden floor. Sophie watched the back of his feet as they swung in a mesmerizing motion as she tried to untangle her encounter with Mr. Argenton.

Something had worried him so badly that he'd sought her out. She knew almost nothing about him, but what she did know convinced her that he wouldn't look that anxious over a trivial problem.

What was wrong, then? Sophie hadn't heard any sort of commotion in the building. But she thought Mr. Argenton might not like her being left alone, which was why he'd suggested she sit with Elise until he returned. Was he worried about someone in the house? Was he worried about what Rose might do?

Rose isn't going to do anything. She is a cultured, intelligent woman. These little…events…are power plays. Once she's comfortable with you, everything will be fine. Just be careful not to upset her.

That presented another problem, though. Sophie raised a hand to where Mr. Argenton had brushed her hair back, and a small glow of pleasure lit deep in her chest. *What would Rose do if I ignored her command? He's my husband. Surely, no one could expect me to reject him if he wanted to spend time with me. Surely…*

Sophie realized too late that the butler had stopped, and nearly walked into him. She jerked back, and embarrassment flooded her face with color, but the butler graciously pretended not to notice. His gaze was focused on somewhere behind her head, and he extended a hand toward the open door.

Inside was the most magnificent library Sophie had ever seen. Shelves, all filled with books, covered nearly every wall and stretched high toward the ceiling. Sophie stepped inside the room, mouth open in wonder, then turned back to the butler. "Thank you."

He was already gone, his shoes clicking quietly as he returned to the stairs. Sophie turned back to the library to absorb the sight. She imagined she could spend many happy hours there. Large, plush chairs were propped in the corners, and a counter—designed for research, she guessed—stretched across one wall. A blaze in the fireplace spread a gentle glow over the room.

She paused to read some of the titles and frowned. *Treaties of the Dead. The Paranormal and the Damned. Legends, Myths, and the Supernatural. The Dead Who Walk.*

There looked to be hundreds of books like those. *What a*

macabre collection. Sophie remembered a book from her own childhood, and the golden words that had been embossed on its stained cover flashed across her mind. *Cryptids and the Occult.* She shook herself away from the memory and moved deeper into the library, suddenly eager to have company.

She found Elise sitting cross-legged on the floor, surrounded by papers. "Good morning, Elise." *Wait, is it still morning? Or has it passed noon now?*

Elise didn't respond. A piece of charcoal was clasped in her hand, and she pulled it across the paper in long, even strokes. Sophie moved closer to examine the pictures and picked up the nearest one.

It drew a gasp from her. Rendered on the paper was a creature she couldn't fully comprehend. Shaped something like a hunched, lanky human, it loomed out of deep shadows. Its open mouth showed white fangs, and its fingers were tipped with fifteen-inch nails. Instead of giving it eyes, Elise had left round, white holes in the elongated head, giving it the appearance of having lamps set in its head.

Sophie dropped the paper as though it had burned her, and she looked at the other drawings with growing dread. Every single piece of paper showed the creature, always staring toward the viewer, always obscured in heavy darkness.

Calm down. It might be some horror she's invented for a story or a play. Ask her; you'll see. "Elise, what is this?"

Elise raised her head. Her eyes fixed on Sophie's face, but they were unfocussed, and her jaw was slack. "He whispers to me."

Her voice was quiet but as clear as a bell. "He watches me at night. I know he does."

Sophie stepped backward. Her legs bumped into a chair, and she collapsed into the leather seat, too shaken to stand. *Is she unwell? Is this normal for her?*

Thunder rumbled, and at last, the rain began to fall. Large, heavy drops hit the windows and slapped against the walls. The thunder seemed to have startled Elise, and she blinked furiously. Some awareness returned to her eyes. She and Sophie stared at each other for a second, then Elise said, "You look very pretty today."

"Oh." Sophie struggled to smile and pressed a hand to her heart. "Thank you. You do, as well."

Like the day before, Elise wore a practical but well-made dress and a ribbon in her black hair. Rather than responding to the compliment, she stood and went to take a seat opposite Sophie. She walked over the drawings without seeming to notice they were there, and the paper crinkled under her boots.

"You—your pictures—" Sophie managed.

"I'll burn them," Elise said calmly as she took her seat. "I always do."

"You…draw often?"

Elise folded her hands in her lap, like a perfect miniature adult, and looked out the window. For the first time, Sophie had the chance to see the girl clearly. There was something wrong about her sunken eyes. At first, Sophie thought they might hold the same deadness as her mother's, but then she realized it was almost the opposite. Elise's eyes were *haunted*.

What happened to her? Has someone hurt her? Her mother—
Sophie remembered the manic glint in Rose's eyes as she'd
stroked the new dresses in Sophie's wardrobe. Again, she had a
horrible premonition that Rose could be capable of a lot more
than appearances suggested.

As she watched the girl sitting silently, Sophie felt pain build
in her chest. She couldn't imagine what had been done to Elise,
but she felt a desperate need to ensure it never happened again.

"It's raining." Elise's gaze was still fixed on the window. "I hate
the rain. It wakes things that are better left asleep."

"Slugs," Sophie agreed. "And snails. They destroy my family's
garden every time it rains."

A very thin smile flittered across Elise's face. "Yes, those, too."

Should I say something about the drawings? "Elise—"

Thunder cracked, and it ran through the house like shivers.
The windows rattled in their panes, and a burst of cold air rushed
down the chimney. The fire hissed then sputtered out a heartbeat.
The lamps lit around the walls held on for a moment more, but
one at a time, they flickered and died.

Sophie gasped and half rose out of her chair. The sky was
incapable of lighting the room; without the lamps, she was as
good as blind. "Elise, are you all right?"

Elise sighed. There was something unsettling about the noise,
as though the very exhalation were filled with deep sadness.

Another thunderclap rattled the window a second time. In
the brief instant of illumination that accompanied the lightning, Sophie caught sight of Elise's face, pale and drawn, her

dark eyes fixed on Sophie as an unhappy frown scrunched her brows together. Then the darkness, thick and cold, rushed back around them.

"Elise?" Sophie repeated, her voice a whisper. No reply. She became aware of movement. Footsteps, slow and even, came from near Elise's seat and arced across the room. Sophie wanted to move away, but fear turned her legs to bricks and froze her to the chair. She gripped the armrests until her fingers ached. The steps came closer, crunching over the discarded pages.

Sophie tried to speak, but her mouth was so dry the words came out as a rasp. "Elise, please answer me."

The footsteps stopped at her side. She could feel a presence there, huge, somehow, and towering over her. It exhaled. The sound was a low rasp in her ear. Sophie squeezed her eyes closed as she broke out in a cold sweat and shivers clawed their way down her back.

Then with a fizzle, the fireplace caught alight. It was only a handful of embers, but the golden glow provided just enough light for Sophie to see the closer parts of the room.

Elise was still in her chair, her eyes cold as she watched Sophie. The library was otherwise empty.

Sophie drew a shuddering breath, lost for words. She released her grip on the armrests and stared at her hands. They were shaking.

"Does he whisper to you, too?" Elise asked.

CHAPTER 13
SECRETS AND LIES

ELISE RETURNED HER ATTENTION to the window as Sophie staggered out of her chair, willing her legs to take her weight. The blackness, barely relieved by the embers, pressed around her. *I have to get out of here.*

She took a step, and one of the pages, scattered by the gust of wind, crumpled under her feet. The charcoal creature's lamp-like eyes stared up at her, eager and hungry. Sophie moved past it as quickly as she could, but stopped at the door.

I have to know.

"Elise…you felt it, too, didn't you?"

The girl's face was blank as she watched the rain stream down the glass. Her eyes were unfocussed again. Sophie shuddered and pushed out of the library, no longer wanting to have anything to do with the magnificent bookcases or their ancient, arcane books.

I need company. I need…

Mr. Argenton. He was the only person in the house she felt safe with. And he was out in the storm, *hunting*.

"Lies," Sophie muttered to herself as she picked up her skirts and rushed down the red-and-gold hallway. She couldn't stop shaking, so she took the energy the fear gave her and turned it into action. *This house is nothing but lies and secrets. I feel like I haven't heard an honest word since I arrived.*

She turned the corner and, mercifully, found the staircase not far ahead of her. She took it to the ground floor and hesitated in the foyer. Shifting sounds came from one of the rooms to her left, and she pushed open the door.

Hopes of finding Mr. Argenton were dashed as the butler straightened. He stood in some sort of storage room, where rows of guns and ammunition lined the walls. The butler held one of the rifles, apparently checking it for defects. Sophie took an impulsive half step away.

The butler fixed his eyes on a place a little above her head. "How may I help, Mrs. Argenton?"

"I, uh… Has Mr. Argenton returned, please?"

"I'm afraid not as of yet. If you like, there is a sitting room that overlooks the front porch."

"Please."

The butler stepped out of the room and indicated a smaller door past the dining room. Sophie gave a small nod of thanks and hurried toward it.

"Mrs. Argenton." The butler's call halted her just as she

reached toward the handle. Sophie turned back to him, and he gestured to his own face. "You have something on your cheek."

"Oh, I'm sorry. I mean—thank you." Sophie pushed into the sitting room, shut the door behind herself, and pressed her back to the cold wood. A fire had been lit, but it was growing low in the grate. Sophie hated the way the shadows fluttered among the corners of the room and behind the furniture, and she hurried to throw a fresh log on the flames.

She looked about the room as the fire spat and hissed at the wood. As with the rest of the house, it was decorated beautifully. A mirror was fixed on the opposite wall, and Sophie went to it. The butler had been right; some dark liquid had dripped onto her left cheek. Sophie smudged it away and frowned at its strangely viscous, tacky texture. She didn't like the feel of it, and wiped her hand and cheek clean on her handkerchief.

The sitting room had one large window facing the front lawn. She could see the stairs leading to the entryway, but the heavy rain hid the woods and lake from her view. Sophie sat in the chair beside the window then wrapped her arms around her torso as she stared into the downpour.

There was something in that room with us. It was too large to be Elise, and I would have heard the door open if anyone else had entered.

Anxiety clawed at her chest again. She felt helpless, like a pawn cornered by rooks, bishops, and one very dangerous queen.

I can't stay in this house. I can't leave. They won't tell me their secrets, and I'm afraid to even ask.

Fresh lightning lit up the lawn. Sophie made out a dark shape in the distance, and she stood. By the time she'd pressed her face to the window, though, the darkness had swallowed up the figure. *Was that Mr. Argenton?*

She returned to the foyer and crossed the marbled expanse to the kitchen. The workers froze when she pushed open the door, but quickly resumed their tasks when they saw it was only Sophie. She hovered in the doorway, trying to catch someone's attention, but they seemed to be trying not to look at her.

"E-excuse me…" She caught at one of the scullery maid's sleeves, halting the girl. The maid looked chagrined at being chosen and fixed her eyes on her feet. "Mr. Argenton is return-ing. Would you fetch us tea and some towels, please?"

The maid didn't reply—*they never seem to unless they have to*—but bobbed in a curtsy and hurried away. Sophie returned to the foyer to wait.

It didn't take long for Mr. Argenton to come in. He was drenched; rivulets of rain ran from his flattened hair and coursed down his cheeks. He seemed to have protected the gun under a thick cloth, which he discarded as he closed the door behind himself.

He hadn't seen her, and Sophie took the chance to examine his face. It was creased with worry lines, and his eyes, normally so cold, swam with dark frustration. Then he looked up and saw her, and a surprised smile washed away the worry. "Sophie, I hope you weren't waiting for me."

"I asked the maid to fetch some towels," Sophie said, forcing herself to keep her voice level. "I don't know if she actually will or not—"

"She will. They're well trained."

The butler had appeared out of the shadows, and Mr. Argenton passed his gun and coat off. Sophie tried not to stare at the way his wet shirt stuck to his chest. The sinewy muscles were outlined clearly and shifted with each breath. She pulled herself free, turned toward the sitting room, and pushed open the door.

"I'll make the furniture wet," Mr. Argenton said. "Give me a few minutes to dry and change."

Please don't leave me alone. "The furniture won't be any worse off here than in your room." Sophie struggled to smile. "And the maid is bringing tea."

Mr. Argenton, who was halfway out of his jacket, froze. His eyes scanned her, lingering on her hesitant smile and shaking hands, then he took a step closer. "Did something happen?"

Sophie opened her mouth to answer but couldn't find any words. Worry lines developed across Mr. Argenton's face. He dropped his jacket on the marble floor and followed Sophie into the sitting room without another word.

CHAPTER 14
QUESTIONS

THE MAID, MOVING QUICKLY and avoiding eye contact, followed them into the room, a tray of tea balanced in one hand and half a dozen towels gripped in the other. She shoved her burdens onto the table, bobbed in the briefest curtsy she could manage, and scurried out of the room.

Mr. Argenton ignored the towels and stepped nearer to Sophie. His wet hand reached toward her arm, but he didn't touch her. When he spoke, his voice was soft but urgent. "What happened? Are you hurt?"

"No," Sophie said quickly. "No, nothing like that. Everything is fine—" *Don't lie to him. Everything is* not *fine.* But Sophie was finding it difficult to maintain her righteous anger now that Mr. Argenton stood so near to her, his black eyes filled with anxiety as they searched her face.

"You're pale. Can I get you anything? Some wine?"

"Thank you, but I'm fine. You—you're dripping on the carpet. Here." Sophie snatched one of the towels off the table and offered it to him. He relaxed a little but continued to watch her out of the corner of his eye as he took the towel and rubbed it through his hair.

"Something happened." The towel moved downward to blot at his shirt, which stuck to his chest.

Sophie caught herself staring at the outlines of his muscles and looked away.

"Are you sure you're all right?"

Sophie busied herself with pouring them both tea as she tried to collect her thoughts. She had Mr. Argenton's attention, and she sensed he wasn't going to try to dodge her questions, so she tried to approach the subject as tactfully as she could. "Elise was drawing some very strange images."

She watched his reaction closely. His eyes fluttered closed for a second, and while he continued to wring the water from his clothes, the motions became automatic, rather than deliberate. He looked away from her, and his voice seemed a little too level when he replied, "I think I can guess—was it a black creature? I hope it didn't alarm you, my dear. Elise has been preoccupied with it for some time."

"Do you have any idea what it is?"

"Some monster she read about in a book, as far as I can gather. She's been having bad dreams about it."

Sophie found that believable. When she was a child, her father had bought her a collection of books from a peddler. Nestled among the fairy tales was a fragile, crumbling text titled *Cryptids and the Occult.* The monsters contained between those pages had fueled Sophie's nightmares for months. She could very easily imagine Elise, already a little maladjusted, picking an ill-judged book off the library shelves and becoming obsessed with its contents.

That didn't explain the presence she'd felt, though. Sophie opened her mouth to ask Mr. Argenton about it, but broke off as he flinched.

He'd been trying to use his left hand to reach his back then quickly switched the towel to his right, turning his body to hide his left arm—but not before Sophie saw red seeping through the sleeve. "You're hurt!"

"I'm fine." He sighed, turning further to block her view. "A branch scratched me while I was hunting; that's all."

A sick, frightened feeling rose in the pit of Sophie's stomach. She moved around to Mr. Argenton's side and took his hand before he could protest. She pushed his sleeve back as carefully as she could. He'd wrapped a strip of cloth around his forearm, but blood was soaking through it. *So this was why he wanted to go to his room before talking with me.*

"It looks serious," she said, refusing to let Mr. Argenton pry her hands away. "We should summon the surgeon. Who do you normally send—"

"The surgeon doesn't like to make house calls to Northwood," Mr. Argenton said.

Sophie raised her head to see his face and was struck, once again, by just how tall her husband was.

Amusement twisted his mouth. "Besides, it would take him nearly half a day to arrive. Trust me, dear Sophie, it looks far worse than it is."

Dear Sophie. She looked away before he could see the color rise to her face. "Do you have a medicine kit?"

"Yes, I'll dress it myself in a moment."

Sophie released his hand and hurried to the door. She was relieved to see the butler was still in the foyer, attempting to wring the water from Mr. Argenton's jacket with the help of a footman. "Please, Mr. Argenton is hurt. Could you bring the medicine kit and some boiled water?"

The butler gave a slow nod and turned toward the kitchen. Sophie returned to Mr. Argenton, who was watching her with faint amusement. "Please, don't let this upset you. It just needs binding, and I can do that myself."

"No." Sophie moved the tea set from the table to the mantel. She then unfolded one of the towels. "My uncle is a doctor. He's taught me how to treat wounds. They need to be washed with boiled water and wrapped in c-clean bandages or they b-become i-infected a-and—"

Mr. Argenton came up behind her and placed his hands on her shoulders. His fingers were cold from the rain, but beautifully gentle as they caressed her skin. Sophie fought with herself to hold back the tears that choked her voice and threatened to spill over her eyes.

"My dear," Mr. Argenton sighed. "*Sophie.* I promise, nothing bad is going to happen. Don't be afraid."

He kissed the top of her head as he stroked her arms. It was an intimate, but not romantic, expression. It was intended to comfort, and Sophie felt herself melting back against him. Even though his shirt was still damp, the heat from his chest radiated through it. When she closed her eyes, she felt safe.

Mr. Argenton. The name echoed in her mind, drowning out the anxious chatter. *Mr. Argenton. No, Joseph.*

The door behind them opened. Joseph sighed as he released Sophie and stepped away from her. She had to blink at the butler and his burden of a large wooden box for a moment before she remembered what she'd requested and why.

"Oh, on the table, please. Thank you."

A maid followed the butler and left a jug of steaming water and a bowl. Sophie waited until the door was closed before turning back to her husband. She congratulated herself on keeping her voice steady when she said, "Take off your shirt, please."

Joseph raised his eyebrows. He looked surprised, but also faintly entertained. "None of this is necessary. This isn't the first time I've cut myself while hunting. If you step outside, I'll take care of it and join you in a few minutes."

Sophie couldn't take her eyes off the makeshift bandage around his arm. It was almost entirely crimson. *How much blood has he lost?* "Do you have any medical training? I do." *A little. When I was eight.* "Please, let me help you."

He watched her carefully, and Sophie saw amusement and curiosity flicker through his eyes before he answered, "You're not going to let me escape, are you?"

"No. Take your shirt off, please."

"I draw the line there," Joseph said, raising a hand to silence her protests. "You can tend it very well with my shirt on."

"Not easily. Not without cutting your sleeve." Something about Joseph's protest rang false. Sophie suspected he had an ulterior motive for staying clothed, and she didn't like what it boded. *What if the cut on his arm isn't the extent of his injury? What if he's hiding worse?*

"Cut it, then. I'm already doubtful about being able to remove the stain."

Sophie stepped closer. The tears were threatening to return, and she used them to her advantage as she blinked at her husband. "*Joseph. Please.*"

He closed his eyes and sighed. "I fell while I was hunting; it's not something I want you to see."

That was what she'd been afraid of. Sophie took a half step nearer, closing the distance between them. "I need you to trust me."

They stared at each other for a moment, in a silent battle of wills, then Joseph grudgingly unbuttoned his shirt and shed it. Sophie pressed a hand over her mouth. Dark, mottled bruises spread across his chest, and a scabbed scratch extended from his collarbone and over his ribs.

Joseph's face darkened as he watched her reaction. "It's not as bad as it looks."

She didn't trust herself to reply, so instead, Sophie indicated for him to take a seat by the fireplace. She was glad she'd put the extra log on it while she was waiting for him; the fire had grown hot and would at least remove his chill. She then pulled the second seat closer to his, poured part of the steaming water into the bowl, and took it and a towel back to her chair.

"You're not afraid of blood?" Joseph asked as she began working his bandage off with trembling fingers. Sophie shook her head, and he smiled at her. "Then you're braver than many women."

His smile, though faint, was infectious, and Sophie smiled back. "I doubt Rose would mind, either."

"Ha. No, I've yet to see Rose disturbed by anything. She has an iron constitution."

Sophie didn't reply, and Joseph's smile faltered as he read into the silence. "Has Rose been causing trouble?"

Yes. "No, of course not. She's been…a very gracious—"

Sophie had managed to get Joseph's bandage off. The jagged cut below was nearly as long as her hand. Her stomach clenched, but she managed to keep her face calm as she dipped a corner of the towel into the bowl of water.

Joseph continued to watch her as Sophie pressed the wet cloth to the injury. She knew it had to hurt him, but he didn't flinch. "Are you certain you're all right, my dear?"

"Yes. Keep still, please." *This wasn't caused by a branch. What, then? A wolf?* She glanced at the scratch on his chest. Three long, straight lines suggested it had also been caused by claws. *Why would he be hunting wolves? Surely not for sport, if he returns with injuries such as these.*

"Sophie." Joseph seemed to be phrasing himself carefully. "I know my aunt can sometimes become…intense. She has some strongly held beliefs and doesn't like having her house altered. But you're my wife, and this is your home now. If Rose ever…" He paused, and Sophie could almost read the words running through his mind—*threatens, commands, daunts*—before he settled on, "If she ever becomes overbearing, tell me."

"Thank you." Sophie had cleaned the blood away from the cut, but it was still red. She opened the medicine chest and sorted through it. She found the ethanol in a brown bottle and poured a liberal amount onto a clean cloth before pressing it to Joseph's arm. A hiss escaped between his clenched teeth, but he kept still.

"Sorry."

"Hah." He relaxed back in his chair as the burn subsided. "Don't be. I haven't had anyone care for me like this since my mother—" The smile flickered out like a snuffed candle, and he continued quickly. "I'm grateful, Sophie."

She discarded the pink-tinged cloth and picked a healing balm out of the box. His offer of protection against Rose lingered with her, but she wasn't sure she was the one who needed it most. As she began wrapping a fresh bandage over the cut, she said, "I'm worried for Elise."

They'd come full circle. Joseph watched her carefully. "What concerns you?"

"How long has she been drawing this creature?"

"Two months."

"And before then—was she showing any signs of maladjustment?"

"She has always been different from other children."

"Is there anything we can do to help her?"

A smile twisted Joseph's mouth. It was worlds away from the soft expressions he occasionally showed her, though; it was bitter and angry. "I've been trying, my dear, but sometimes, it feels as though every step I take is a mistake."

Sophie finished tying the bandage and let her hands rest on his arm. The fire had warmed him enough that his skin no longer felt cold. "I'll help," she said. "You're not alone anymore."

She wasn't sure what had prompted her to say it, except that, from the very little she knew about Joseph, he struck her as a lonely man. His eyes flicked to her, surprised, then filled with gratitude. His other hand rose to her cheek and stroked where the fire had colored her skin pink.

"Joseph…"

A log shifted in the fireplace, sending up sparks, and Sophie flinched. Joseph felt the motion, and concern darkened his eyes. "What is it?"

The shifting wood had brought back the memory of the brief moments in the library when the fire had been extinguished and a presence had moved through the room. Sophie squeezed her eyes closed. *Ask him now.* "Joseph, do you believe in ghosts?"

CHAPTER 15
GHOSTS

HIS HAND LINGERED ON her cheek, but the fingers stiffened. When he didn't answer, Sophie opened her eyes and saw the cold anxiety had returned to his face. *He knows there are spirits in Northwood.*

He wet his lips before asking, "What happened?"

Sophie, very haltingly, told him about the presence she'd heard approach her. Joseph withdrew his hand and pressed it over his mouth as he scowled at the fire. He didn't speak for several minutes after she'd finished, but his pale, angular face had regained its cool expression. Sophie tried, and failed, to guess what he was thinking.

At last, in a clipped voice, he said, "Very old houses often retain impressions of their occupants. Generally, the beings are benign or even welcoming."

"Are Northwood's ghosts welcoming?"

"Don't be frightened of them" was Joseph's evasive answer.

"They're only spirits; they can't harm you. They're generally restful, as well—I wouldn't be surprised if your experience today is as much as you'll see of them for the year."

His words weren't as comforting to Sophie as he clearly wanted them to be. She thought of the house, huge and foreboding, with its shadows so heavy that she could almost inhale them. Did she have to share the maze-like passageways with spirits, too? How many were there?

If the Argentons had lived in the house for generations, the spirits could be Joseph's ancestors. Were they just as opposed to her presence as Rose was?

She'd read a little about ghosts in the book her father had erroneously bought her. She wished she could remember more than she did. There had been something about how the spirits only remained on earth after a traumatic life or violent death. One of the illustrations had haunted her dreams; it had been of a wealthy, upper-class woman standing over the body of her sister, an ax clasped in her hand, as the unfortunate sister's head rolled about her feet. The caption had read: *the making of a vengeful ghost.*

Sophie leaned closer to the fire, suddenly feeling cold. She thought about Rose's bizarre intensity and how Joseph reminded her of a hungry wolf. How much blood had been shed in Northwood? And what stopped the spirits from moving on to the next life?

"My dear." Joseph's voice interrupted her thoughts. "You're upset. That wasn't my intention."

Sophie managed to smile, then her eyes dropped to his chest.

The lean muscles hinted at tremendous strength, even with the discoloration. She flushed and cleared her throat. "I forgot, you have another cut—"

"Don't mind that one." Joseph rose from the chair and picked up his shirt before Sophie could argue. "It's already half healed."

Looking at it again, Sophie saw it was several days old. It had scabbed over, and the skin was already knitting together in places. Anything she did would only reopen the cuts.

Joseph's shirt had dried in the heat of the fire, and he pulled it on and buttoned it quickly. "Lunch will be served in an hour, but I have some urgent business to attend to first. Will you be all right until then?"

Sophie glanced toward the door leading to the foyer, beyond which the house stretched away like a black labyrinth. Then she looked at the window, which was still drenched by the heavy rain. She opened her mouth to say yes, but the word died on her lips.

Joseph stroked a hand over her arm. "Dear Sophie," he said, and she found herself leaning into his touch. "Don't think I'm insensible to your situation. I know Northwood is a grim substitute for your old life. But I believe you can be happy here."

"Maybe…" Sophie hesitated, then cleared her throat. "Maybe we could take a room in the city—"

"Northwood is our home. I don't wish to leave it."

"Yes." Sophie tried not to let her despair show.

Joseph sighed, took her hand, and kissed the fingertips. "This move has been difficult for you. Let me help. Tell me something you would enjoy, and I'll give it to you if it's within my power."

Sophie stared at the large, gentle hand that held hers. *Something I'd enjoy…to be away from Northwood. But I can't ask for that; he's already made it clear it's not an option.* "A picnic," she settled on at last. She'd loved having picnics when her family visited the parks.

Surprise drew Joseph's eyebrows up, and pleasure twitched at the corners of his lips. "Certainly. Would you like the whole family to join, or—"

"Just us," Sophie said quickly, imagining how Rose might react. "Just you and me."

"Let's have it early tomorrow, then. I have business in town in the afternoon, so we'll make it a breakfast picnic."

Sophie started, and the anxiety, held at bay over the previous minutes, reared its head. "You're leaving?"

"Only for half a day. It was business I was hoping could be deferred until later this week, but it's become too urgent to delay any longer. I'll be back by dinner."

Half a day alone with Rose, with the house, the servants who never speak or look at me unless they have to, Elise's drawings, and the spirits…

"Sophie?"

She forced a smile. "Of course I'll be fine. Half a day is nothing."

He kissed her hand again. "Would you like me to show you to your room?"

"Thank you, but I'd better become familiar with the way myself."

"Then I'll see you at dinner." His thumb ran across the back of her fingers a final time, then he left the room at a brisk pace.

Sophie watched the fire for a long time. Now that she was alone, the small noises of the house returned to her: the crackle of burning wood, the quiet roar of the rain as it drenched the mansion, the clatters and muffled voices coming from the kitchen, and in the distance, animal noises and the groan of shifting trees.

My house is haunted.

It sounded like such a ridiculous phrase, but Sophie could no longer doubt its truth. Joseph had confirmed her suspicions, and he wasn't the sort of person who could be caught up by a flight of fancy. If he acknowledged the spirits, then there could be no doubt about their existence.

Can I live in a haunted house?

Joseph had for his entire life, Sophie reminded herself. And most likely Rose and Garrett Argenton, as well. *But can I?*

Maybe, if...

Something had been growing in Sophie since the previous evening, but she barely dared admit it to herself. *I think I love him.* It felt like a tiny, helpless, fluttering emotion that could be squashed in a heartbeat. But it grew stronger with every passing moment, every word he said to her, every touch, and every time his eyes, so dark and intense, fixed on her. She loved him. And she thought he at least liked her back.

Rose wants me to stay away from Joseph. But now I don't think I could, even if I wanted to. And I don't. I should be able to enjoy my husband's company, no matter what Rose thinks.

Sophie couldn't keep still any longer and strode to the window. The lightning had spent itself, but the rain continued to lash against the building. A small, delighted smile took over Sophie's face as she watched the water cascade down the panes. *I love him. I almost can't believe it.*

A shape, slouched so far over that its torso was nearly parallel with the ground, slunk across the lawn. Sophie clasped a hand over her mouth to smother her shriek. Even before she was able to get a proper look at the figure, it had passed by the light of the window and disappeared into the rain. Every good, happy feeling within her evaporated in a snap.

That wasn't human.

Sophie's heart beat so hard that it was painful. She backed away from the window, terrified of seeing the shape's return but incapable of looking away. The sitting room, which had felt cozy before, seemed horribly dim. The fire had consumed almost all of the wood she'd thrown in, and darkness clawed its way in from the corners and crevices.

At that moment, Sophie wanted company more than anything else in the world. Joseph had said he had urgent work to do, and she worried he might become frustrated if she disturbed him. She couldn't sit with Rose or Garrett Argenton, and her earlier experience with Elise had been less than comforting.

Of course—Marie. I can call her with the excuse of changing for lunch. I'm sure she'd sit with me a while if I asked her.

Sophie rushed from the sitting room and took the stairs two at a time. She felt vulnerable as long as she was under the vast, vaulted ceiling, and she longed for the relative safety of her room.

She hesitated when she reached the third floor. *My room is to the right, isn't it?*

A door closed behind her, and Sophie turned to see Rose standing in the shadowed passageway. The other woman's eyes shone eerily in the candlelight, and her mouth was set in a hard line.

She knows, Sophie realized, her heart sinking, and took an impulsive step backward. *She knows I spent the last two hours with Joseph.*

Rose moved forward slowly and stopped at the other side of the stairs. She held something small and white in her hands, but it took Sophie a moment to realize what it was. *My letter!*

"Stay away from him." Rose's voice was disturbingly even and cool, and the words were spoken clearly, so that each one hit Sophie like a blow. "I won't warn you again."

Rose raised the letter and tore it in half. Sophie inhaled sharply and reached toward it, but she was too late. Rose placed the halves on top of each other, tore them again, then repeated the process twice more. When she opened her hands, little squares of paper fluttered to the floor. Rose didn't wait for Sophie to speak, but crossed to the stairs, her boots scraping over the torn letter, and descended out of sight.

Sophie clenched her fists at her side and blinked her wet eyes. She'd been punished for her transgression, and it was a steep punishment indeed. She could write another letter—that wouldn't be a problem—but Rose's message had been clear: she was cutting off contact between Sophie and her family.

I could send my letters through Joseph instead. He should be able to take one when he goes to town tomorrow. But would I ever receive a reply? Rose or one of her helpers would intercept them before they made it past the front door. Hateful, horrible woman.

CHAPTER 16
THE ROOM

SOPHIE RUSHED THROUGH THE halls, guessing the way to her room. She would have to face Rose again at the lunch table, but she could at least enjoy half an hour of Marie's company before then. Sophie took a right then a left, but found herself at the servant's stairwell. Retracing her steps, she tried following the original passageway farther before turning off. That only brought her to a dead end. She turned back and tried a different offshoot.

The new hallway was lined with paintings she thought she recognized. The portraits all showed black-haired, dark-eyed men and women. *Joseph's ancestors. Do any of them continue to walk these hallways?*

She took another right, then froze as she realized which hallway she'd entered. The wallpaper had changed to black and gold, and the hall contained no exits except for the single, imposing red door set at its end.

Sophie made to turn away then stopped. Some kind of whispering noise seemed to come from beyond the door.

Joseph said not to go through it. And you decided to trust Joseph, didn't you?

The door handle twitched. The motion was so small that Sophie almost could have sworn she'd imagined it.

Do I still trust him even when he lies to me? He wasn't going hunting this morning, and those cuts weren't made by branches.

Sophie had started walking toward the door without even realizing it.

He's keeping secrets. Is it really so wrong to want to uncover them?

Her fingers hovered over the handle. It felt cold, much colder than anything else in the house. The whispering sound was louder—almost, but not quite loud enough for her to make out the words. Her fingers brushed over the metal as she battled with herself. Then she drew a long, shuddering breath and pulled her hand back. *Joseph is all I have right now. I need to trust he has my best interests at heart.*

She turned to the hallway and gasped. Two black eyes set in a pale face glared at her from the shadows. Red lips parted in a frustrated sneer, then Rose turned and swept away with a swirl of her black dress.

Sophie pressed a hand to her thundering heart. *What was she doing there? Did she follow me?* She waited just long enough to be sure Rose was gone before she hurried down the hallway and took the opposite direction. Frustration and embarrassment made tears prick at her eyes. *I can't even walk through this house without being watched. Does she want me to go through the door? Is she hoping I'll fall through a rotten floorboard and die? If that's even the reason why the door is forbidden...*

Strands of her hair had fallen free from its design, and Sophie brushed them away from her face furiously. Either there were no maids on that floor, or they were hiding from her; she didn't pass a single soul in the maze. Anxiety rose as she searched for familiar landmarks with increasing desperation. At last, she stopped in the middle of a wide, unfamiliar passageway, breathing heavily and clenching her hands to stop them from shaking.

Calm down. You can't get lost inside a house. Eventually, you'll find your way back.

Sophie turned in a circle, examining the hallway. The wallpaper was identical to every other part of that floor, but she didn't recognize the paintings. She wrung her hands, trying to guess a direction, then jolted as the door opposite her creaked open.

"H-hello?"

There was no answer. The door drew inward, revealing a small, square room. A table sat in its center, with a single lit candle on top. Otherwise, the room was bare.

Sophie took a step toward it. "Hello?"

If it's one of the maids, she might not answer me. But I need directions—it's got to be close to lunch.

She crept closer to the open frame. The door continued to glide inward until it hit the wall and rebounded an inch before falling still.

"Please, is someone in here?"

Not daring to enter the room, she stopped at the threshold, her feet still in the hallway, and bent forward to see into the room's corner.

Something large and cold hit her back. The blow wasn't hard—it felt no more substantial than a gust of wind—but it had enough force to throw her to the floor inside the room. Sophie gasped as the fall jarred her, then she rolled onto her back. The doorway was empty.

She scrambled to get to her feet, but the door rushed closed, slamming into its frame with so much force that the wood shook. Sophie ran to it, but the handle wouldn't turn.

"Hello!" Her voice rang shrilly in her ears as she tugged at the handle and clawed at the door's lock. "Hello, please, I need help!"

Silence. The handle held as though it had been welded into place.

A quiet footstep echoed through the room, and Sophie swung to put the door to her back. She was alone, and yet…

The candle flickered as though someone, or something, had moved past it.

There was nothing in the room to hide a person. The room was entirely bare, even of wall decorations, except for the small round table and its candle.

Sophie felt as though she could collapse, and wedged herself against the door. She drew a shaking breath and wet her lips. "A-are you th-the spirit that i-inhabits this house?"

There was no answer, but Sophie thought the candle flickered slightly. *Don't be frightened. Joseph says they're benign. They can't hurt you.*

"H-hello." She was finding it hard to draw breath, as though the room's air had thickened into an invisible soup. She bowed her head as low as she dared without losing sight of the room. "My n-name is Sophie. I married Jo... Mr. Argenton. Th-thank you for letting me s-stay in your beautiful home."

Again, no answer. Sophie felt behind herself for the door handle and tried it again, but it still stuck.

"If you have s-something to tell me, I'd be glad to listen."

The candle flickered, but otherwise, the room was still.

Something warm tickled the hand that held the handle, and Sophie pulled it away with a gasp. Bright-red liquid ran down her fingers. She rubbed her index finger against her thumb, and revulsion rose in her throat. *It's blood.*

She turned to study the door. Red liquid dripped from around where the metal was fixed to the wood and from inside the keyhole. Sophie took a step away from it, then jolted as something behind her exhaled.

Frightened to lose sight of the door and afraid of turning her back to the room, Sophie rotated on the spot, shivering at the way the shadows flickered in the corners and spread along the roof. "Please, i-if I've done anything to upset you, forgive me. It was n-not intentional."

A drop of blood hit her forearm. Sophie looked to the ceiling and saw dark stains were growing across the plaster. Another drop fell, narrowly missing her, and she retreated to a corner. "I only want to respect you and your home," she said, her voice rising into a frightened, desperate cry. "If you want something, tell me!

If you want me to leave your home, I will! Open the door, and I'll go tonight!"

More drips fell. One hit Sophie's cheek, and she moaned as she shied away from it. The color had spread across the entire ceiling, staining it black. Cracks appeared where the walls met the ceiling, and blood began to ooze from those spaces, running down the wallpaper in thick dribbles.

Sophie couldn't take any more. She ran to the door and began beating her fists on the rapidly dampening surface, screaming as loudly as her voice would allow, "Help! Please, please, someone help!"

The hot liquid dribbled onto her hair, down the back of her neck, and onto her face. Sophie's calls devolved into screams as the smell—heavy, metallic, and sick—filled her nose. The drips increased until they drenched her as thoroughly as if she'd been standing in the storm. It got into her mouth, coating her tongue in its sickening taste. Her ears were full of the quiet pitter-patter of the floor being soaked. The blood ran over her face and burned her eyes.

Something snapped inside her. She screamed as she clawed at the door, scraping her fingertips raw. Tears mingled with the blood running down her face. When she blinked them open, a base, hysterical part of her wanted to laugh at the sight of her dress—the beautiful, elaborate white one Rose had chosen—painted crimson.

She collapsed to the floor, unable to breathe, unable to fight any longer, and unable to do anything except retch at the taste filling her mouth. The blood rain wouldn't stop. The door wouldn't open.

Then a quiet noise disturbed the dripping sounds. To Sophie's panicked, frantic mind, it seemed like feet sliding across the wet floor, pacing around the table, and moving toward her.

Sophie raised her hands over her head, trying to block the noise out and shield her face. She tried to draw a breath, but the air stuck in her throat. Her head swam, and her heart, taxed beyond endurance, felt frozen.

Then a new sound filtered through to her: footsteps, heavy and loud, thundering down the hallway. A voice yelled, "Sophie!"

Joseph. Sophie dragged herself to her knees. She didn't have enough breath in her lungs to call back. She pressed her hand to the blood-soaked door, silently begging him to find her.

The spirit's footsteps continued past the table, moving nearer.

The door handle rattled, then Joseph beat his fist against it. "Sophie! Answer me!"

"Help," she gasped. She felt as if she were drowning in the downpour, and a rushing sensation filled her head.

The footsteps were almost on top of her. She didn't have enough energy to turn and look at it, even if she'd wanted to, but she could feel it—huge, malevolent, and looming over her.

"Move away from the door," Joseph called, then there was a terrific crack. The door held.

Sophie shrank into a ball and covered her head. The being above her exhaled, and she felt its breath, colder than ice, graze her wet arm.

With another crack, the door splintered. It broke in on the third impact, and Joseph pushed through the doorway, his teeth bared and eyes blazing.

If the sight shocked him, he didn't show it. He crossed to Sophie in a single pace, scooped her off the floor, then cradled her to his chest as he carried her from the room.

As soon as she was back in the hallway, the air's heaviness dissipated. Sophie drew a quick, gasping breath. Her fingers found Joseph's shirt, and she clutched at him.

"You're going to be all right, my darling," he murmured, pulling her closer. "Shh, you'll be all right." Then, in a harsher tone, he barked, "Out of my way. Marie, follow us."

Sophie cracked her eyes open to catch a glimpse of Rose, hands clasped behind her back, slinking to one side to let them pass. The older woman's face was serious, but her dead eyes were filled with macabre delight.

Sophie tilted her head back to see Joseph. His jaw was set in a hard line, and his eyes shone in the dim light as he carried her away from the room. She'd never imagined he could look so angry.

"Don't be frightened, my darling," he whispered in a voice far softer than his expression. "I'm with you. You're safe."

CHAPTER 17
RED

THE FOLLOWING EVENTS WERE a blur. Joseph moved quickly, navigating the labyrinth with familiar ease. A quick tapping sound followed them, and when Sophie opened her eyes to look over Joseph's shoulder, she saw Marie—her round face pale—jogging to keep up with her employer's long strides.

Sophie began shivering as the coating of blood cooled. The bitter taste still filled her mouth. She had no idea where they were going, and she had no energy left to ask. But Joseph held her carefully, her head nestled against his shoulder, and occasionally murmured comforting words.

They stopped in a tiled room Sophie didn't recognize, and Joseph lowered her to the floor. She tightened her grip on his shirt, frightened of being left alone, and he stroked her fingers until they relaxed enough to allow him to pull back. A cup was raised to her lips, and clean water was poured into her mouth.

"Spit," Joseph urged, and she did, finally purging the metallic taste from her tongue.

There were noises all about her. She blinked against the light and saw the room was full of maids bearing towels and buckets of hot water.

Joseph's hand caressed the back of her head, even though it was sticky with congealing blood. "I'm going to step outside while Marie helps you bathe," he said, speaking slowly so that she could understand him through the daze of shock. "I'll return soon."

Sophie wanted to protest, but couldn't find the words. Joseph eased her head back against something hard and cold, and she realized he hadn't placed her on the floor as she'd thought, but into a bathtub.

Both Joseph and the maids left the room. Once the door was safely closed, Marie used scissors to cut away the blood-soaked dress and threw it into a pail in the corner of the room. She then began pouring the steaming water over Sophie.

Sophie felt numb. The water prickled at her skin and stung her scraped fingertips, but she couldn't feel its heat.

Marie kept pouring the water carefully, paying special attention to Sophie's hair, then she drained the bathtub and started the process again. Eventually, she took up a scrubbing brush and added soap. The task seemed to take hours, though later, Sophie guessed it couldn't have been more than forty minutes until the bathtub, finally full of clear water, was drained for the last time.

Her legs felt as though they were made of paper, but Marie

helped her stand and dressed her in a nightgown. Then she sat Sophie on a chair and went to the door.

Joseph entered again and knelt before Sophie. "How are you feeling?"

She thought she gave him a crooked smile.

He wrapped his arms around her and prepared to lift her, but Sophie pushed him back. "I can walk." *Is that my voice? I sound so old.*

"Lean on me, then," Joseph said, helping her to stand.

The tile floor was cold under her feet, but Joseph wrapped a warm arm around her shoulders. Marie opened the door for them, and Joseph led Sophie out of the bathroom, down the hallway, and through another door. He kept the pace slow and careful, but she could feel his darkly anxious eyes on her.

Once the door closed behind them, Sophie looked up and realized he'd brought her to her own room. He helped her into bed, wrapped the blankets about her, then retrieved a tray of tea from her writing desk.

"I brought laudanum to help you sleep." He poured two drinks; one of plain tea and one of the narcotic. He left them both on the bedside table then pulled up a chair to sit near her.

He didn't talk or ask questions, but let Sophie stare at the ceiling in silence as she collected herself. The numb feeling was beginning to fade, and in its place, a horrible ache settled in her chest. A single thought had become lodged in her mind, and she found she couldn't move past it.

"You lied to me," she said at last. "You told me they were benign."

Joseph dropped his head and exhaled heavily. "I'm so sorry."

Sophie struggled to sit up. Every muscle in her body felt sore. Joseph leaned forward to prop a pillow behind her back, and as he reached around her, she felt the heat radiating from him. She closed her eyes, and it was all she could do to stop herself from pulling him closer.

He feels so warm and safe.

Joseph sat back in his chair and offered her the drinks. The tea was growing cold, but she was thirsty and drank it, followed by the laudanum. Joseph waited until she'd placed both cups back on the bedside table before saying, "I've tried to find a way to express my profound and crushing regret about what happened tonight, but words are wholly inadequate. Sophie, my darling. You must hate me."

"I don't." She couldn't bring herself to meet his eyes, staring at her interlaced fingers instead.

A bitter "Ha!" escaped Joseph, then he said, so quietly that she doubted it was intended for her to hear, "You should. Sometimes, I wish you did."

Sophie didn't know what to say.

Joseph continued, "I shouldn't have left you alone."

"You had urgent work."

"Nothing that's more important than your safety. And I'm sorry I couldn't reach you sooner. I was at almost the opposite side of the house, and noise travels poorly through the rooms. Marie heard you and ran to fetch me. I couldn't understand what she was miming, so she nearly dragged me from my room."

Sophie managed a smile at that. "I'll have to thank her tomorrow."

Joseph nodded toward the empty cups. "Would you like more tea? Or can I bring you anything else—wine or more blankets?"

"No, I'm better now. Thank you." The ache was a crushing pressure in her chest, but she could at least think clearly. "You'll take me away from Northwood, won't you? Can we go at first light?"

He didn't reply, and Sophie was compelled to look at him. She'd thought his black eyes were emotionless when they'd first met, but she was starting to realize how wrong she'd been. They were shuttered, but hidden behind the thin gauze of self-control was a tempest of feelings, hopes, and fears. Once she learned to read them, she realized his eyes were some of the most expressive she'd ever seen. And the resignation reflected at her made her feel physically sick.

"You intend to stay, don't you?" she breathed.

Joseph gave a slow nod. "You won't want to hear this—and with good reason—but yes, I will stay. Understand, my dear, what leaving Northwood would mean for me. It has been my family's home for centuries. My ancestors have stayed through floods, fires, disease, and war—they didn't abandon it even in times of famine."

"You're not your family, though," Sophie said. "You're not obliged to stay, regardless of tradition!"

Joseph made to take her hand, but Sophie pulled it away. A spark of pain flashed through his eyes, then the shutters were put back in place. His voice returned to its cool, emotionless cadence as he leaned back in his chair. "I stay because I choose to. I'm not asking you to understand or empathize with my reasons, but I do ask that you respect them."

"But surely not after what happened—"

"I severely regret what happened, but my anticipation is that it won't repeat. Spirits have limited energy and need time to regain their strength after any kind of dramatic display. That could take years or even decades. And I suspect today's events were an impulsive reaction against what they perceived as a stranger invading their home. Once they're familiar with you, I'm sure they'll have no objections toward your staying."

The tears were burning her eyes. Sophie rolled onto her side, facing away from Joseph, so that he wouldn't see them.

"Sophie." His voice was softer, but held no hint of relenting. "I'm not overlooking what happened. Far from it. But I hope you can grow to become fond of this house in the same way I am. I know you're stronger than you appear; a weak woman would not have bandaged my arm as you did this afternoon. I know you can excel as Northwood's mistress."

Sophie squeezed her eyes closed and fought to keep herself from shaking. She couldn't believe Joseph expected her to stay. How could he ask that of her? Northwood's spirits hated her. They'd made that more than clear. She couldn't live in a building where the very walls revolted against her.

Joseph's hand, large and warm, made to caress her arm, but Sophie flinched away. He sighed, and the sound was mingled frustration and regret. "I don't want us to fight."

She didn't reply.

The silence stretched out for several minutes, then Sophie heard the chair creak as Joseph stood. "You need to rest. We can discuss this more tomorrow, if you wish."

A cold claw of fear squeezed at Sophie's insides as she listened to Joseph move toward the door. Without him, she would be alone. *Just you and the house.* She pushed herself up as the door opened and stretched her hand toward him. "Joseph—"

The lamp cast a harsh light over his features. He looked ghastly, as though the previous hours had aged him prematurely. Dark circles framed his eyes, and the indents in his cheeks were more pronounced. Something powerful sizzled in his eyes as Sophie called to him, though, and he stopped in the doorway. "Would you like me to stay?"

She couldn't find the words to speak, but nodded. Joseph gave her a faint, sad smile, closed the door, and crossed the room to take her outstretched hand in his. "Of course I will. Lie back, now, and rest. Would you like me to stroke your hair until you fall asleep?"

She nodded again, and Joseph's fingers, warm and light as feathers, brushed over her temple and ran across her hair. She closed her eyes and focused on the sensation.

The fragile, fluttering emotion that had been born that afternoon was bruised, but not dead. As Joseph caressed her, she realized, despite everything, and against everything her logic and desire for self-preservation told her, she still loved him.

She'd thought she would struggle to sleep that night, but the laudanum took grip quickly, and she was unconscious before she even realized she was tired.

CHAPTER 18
REPRISE

SOPHIE WOKE DURING THE night. Her mind felt fuzzy and dense, and it took her a moment to realize where she was.

The storm had spent itself, and the clouds had cleared, leaving a full moon to paint over the landscape and give a square of its light to her room.

She rolled over and saw Joseph sleeping in the chair beside her. He rested his head on the arm he'd bent over the chair's back, and he'd crossed his lanky legs under her bed. It didn't look comfortable, and for a moment, Sophie considered waking him. *I don't want him to leave, though.*

Joseph looked peaceful. His breathing was slow and even, and his eyebrows, which she'd become used to seeing constricted in worry, were relaxed.

He's beautiful, she realized. *I never noticed how long his eyelashes were or how soft his hair is.*

She reached a trembling hand toward him and brushed some of his black hair away from his forehead then, as lightly as she could, ran her fingertips down the side of his face.

He stirred, and his lips parted a fraction. Sophie drew back and pressed her hand over her own mouth to hide the embarrassed smile.

Then a note floated to her through the cold night air, and her heart plunged. The melody, slow and twisted, swelled as it swept through Northwood, coursing between the walls and echoing in her bones.

Joseph's eyebrows pulled together, and the hard lines returned to his face, but he didn't wake.

Sophie brought her knees up under her chin and clutched her arms around her legs as she waited for the song to reach its crescendo and break. It seemed to go on for ages, and every note made her feel sick. When it finally finished, she let herself relax back in bed and returned her eyes to Joseph. The stress across his face gradually faded with the last echoes of the music.

Why do you stay in this house? You claim heritage and tradition, but I can't believe that's your only reason. Why would you subject yourself to a building like this?

She felt for the fluttering emotion inside her and found it alive and strong. It had latched on to her heart, and although she knew she would be wise to pry it away and kill it, she couldn't. Despite the lies and secrets, she still loved him, even though it wasn't reciprocated.

She could no longer fool herself into believing his caresses and kind words were anything more than a man attempting to do what he believed a good husband should. If he loved her the way she loved him, he would have taken her away from Northwood. He cared more for a sprawling collection of bricks than for his bride. That knowledge hurt her more than she'd thought was possible.

Unable to watch him any longer, she rolled over. This time, without the laudanum, sleep evaded her for a very long time.

CHAPTER 19
PICNIC BASKETS

WHEN SOPHIE WOKE THE next morning, Joseph was gone. In his place sat Marie. Color had returned to her face, but her eyes were just as wide and anxious as they'd been the night before. She hovered around her mistress, clearly desperate to find a way to help, as Sophie climbed out of the bed. As soon as she had her feet, Sophie pulled Marie into a tight hug.

"Thank you," she said, "for everything you did last night. I can't express how grateful I am."

Marie froze in surprise then wrapped her arms around Sophie and hugged back. Sophie smiled then released Marie with a deep sigh. "I suppose we'd better make me presentable. Will you help me pick a dress?"

As Marie sorted through the rows of ornate gowns in silent rapture, Sophie turned her mind back to her predicament. She needed to get away from Northwood. She hoped Joseph would come with her, but failing that, she needed him to consent to her taking a room in the city.

If she suggested it as a temporary break—just a few weeks spent in the city, until she felt capable of returning to her home— she thought he might just agree. And if she could organize a visit to her family, followed by a visit to her uncle, followed by a visit to some distant friends, it would be very easy for a few weeks to morph into half a year and for half a year to turn into several years, until it seemed completely natural that she was permanently living in the city. She might even be able to convince Joseph to join her after a little while.

Marie held out a rich-blue silk dress, and Sophie nodded. "That's perfect. Thank you, Marie."

As Marie fixed the dress in place, Sophie braced herself for the upcoming battle. She wanted to talk to Joseph somewhere private and comfortable, where they were both on an even footing. She would have suggested the library, with its collection of beautiful shelves and plentiful books, except for what had happened with Elise the day before. *Possibly one of the sitting rooms, then…*

"Marie, do you know where Mr. Argenton is?"

Marie nodded and pointed to the window.

Sophie felt her heart drop as she gazed at the rows of trees encircling their home. Mist hovered around their bases like a shroud, and she could make out the faint sounds of groaning wood. *He's hunting again.* She wet her lips. "How long has he been gone?"

Marie held up two fingers.

"Two hours?"

The maid nodded then mimed at the chair and the door.

"Did he ask you to stay with me when he left?"

After another nod, Sophie felt a little warmth creep back into her. Joseph's consideration boded well. He might not love her, but at least he wasn't completely indifferent to her.

Sophie had Marie fix her hair into a simple style that let it cascade down her back. It created a harsh contrast against Northwood's dark formality. The effect was what Sophie wanted—to look as though she didn't belong there. Sophie turned to leave her room but hesitated at the door. "You hate this house, don't you, Marie?"

Marie made no reply, but a look at her eyes was confirmation enough.

Sophie gave her a grim smile. "I hate it, too. I'm going to try to leave. I'll take you with me, if it's at all possible."

Marie smiled and mimed something that Sophie couldn't understand.

"I'm sorry. I don't—"

Marie shook her head and waved Sophie toward the door, implying she would explain later. She had a curious, excited look about her face, though, and Sophie couldn't help wondering what her maid had planned.

Marie led her to the stairs, and Sophie returned to the sitting room off the foyer to wait for Joseph's return. The towels, jugs of water, and medical kit from the previous day had been cleared away, but Sophie could still picture Joseph sitting by the fire, dark bruises spread across his chest and blood drying in his scratches. *I can't understand it. Why does he like this place? Any other person would hate it. He's wealthy; I'm sure he could afford to move to a more comfortable home, even if he wasn't able to or didn't want to sell Northwood. He has no reason to linger here.*

The mist was rapidly clearing as the sun breached the top of the trees and spread its heat over the property. There wasn't a single cloud in the sky, but it felt to Sophie like the sun's influence was dampened and dimmed, almost as though it were the heart of winter instead of late spring. Every few minutes she thought she caught some sort of movement among the trees, but the shapes shifted back into the shadows too quickly for her to see if they were deer or some other wood animal.

Why does he have to hunt the wolves? What if one has injured him, and he can't get back to the house? How long should I wait before sending a search party? Could I even convince any of the staff to venture into the woods?

A familiar figure emerged from the forest, and Sophie started out of her chair, relief making it hard to breathe. She pressed close to the window and tried to see if Joseph was injured. If he was, it couldn't have been serious; his strides were long and confident, and he cradled the shotgun over one arm. At one point, he glanced toward a part of the house above Sophie, and she tried to guess what he was looking at. Her heart gave an odd lurch when she realized that her room was approximately where his gaze had been directed.

She patted at her hair to make sure it hadn't come loose, then went into the foyer to wait. The door opened, and Joseph's face brightened with surprise and pleasure when he saw her.

"Sophie." He propped the gun against the door and crossed to her immediately. "How are you?"

"How are *you*?" she countered. "You're not hurt?"

She scanned his limbs for any fresh bandages, and he chuckled. It was a deep and surprisingly pleasant sound, and Sophie felt the heat return to her face.

"Please don't think yesterday's accident was in any way a common occurrence. Don't worry—I won't need any bandages today. But you avoided my question. How are *you*?"

"Much better today. Thank you."

Joseph brushed a lock of hair behind Sophie's ears. She hadn't thought it would be possible to turn any redder, but her face somehow managed it. He was smiling at her, and rather than his usual tight-lipped, half-bitter expression, it was a look of genuine pleasure.

"You should wear your hair down more often," he murmured. "It suits you."

His fingers lingered on her neck, and the plans of wheedling permission to leave Northwood nearly slipped from Sophie's mind. *I would put up with a lot to be near him like this. Could I endure Northwood? I almost think I could.*

"Would you like to have your picnic now?" Joseph asked, startling Sophie out of her thoughts.

"Ah, pardon?"

His smile widened and extended to his eyes. "Yesterday, I promised you a picnic. I thought you might need to spend today resting in your room, but I had the kitchen prepare a basket just in case."

A picnic—outside of Northwood—would be perfect. "Yes, that sounds wonderful. Can we go now?"

"Certainly. Would you like a wrap or a jacket to keep you warm? The sun is bright, but I'm afraid the wind is still chilled."

"Thank you, but I'll be warm enough in this."

"Are you sure? I don't want you to catch cold under my watch."

"Absolutely sure."

"Then let's go."

Sophie hadn't even noticed a maid had appeared at Joseph's side. She held a basket with a blanket wrapped under the handle, which he took in one hand while offering Sophie his other. She took it and followed him through the doors.

CHAPTER 20
THE LAKE

JOSEPH HAD BEEN RIGHT: the sun wasn't quite hot enough to negate the cool wind, but Sophie didn't want to delay the outing to find a shawl. Joseph's arm was warm under hers, and she found herself nestling closer to him as they crossed the lawn.

"I thought we could sit by the lake," Joseph said. "The fish like to come near the surface on sunny days."

"That sounds lovely."

Sophie looked about the property as they approached the water's edge. It was the first time she'd seen it properly since her arrival, and her first impressions—that it seemed dim and strangely unhealthy—were sadly accurate. The grass had an odd gray tint, and the trees, although their branches were full of leaves, looked half-dead. Little landscaping existed around the house, and while Sophie normally enjoyed nature, she found Northwood's grounds unsatisfying and stark. Despite all of that, she was glad to be out of the smothering house, and her companion seemed to be in a good mood.

Joseph threw the blanket over a smooth patch of grass near the lake's edge and helped Sophie onto it. He knelt next to her and began pulling food out of the basket. Sophie hadn't expected it to hold much, but it had been packed tightly. Plates of cold meats followed fresh fruit, cheeses, bread and preserves, sandwiches and pastries. "We can't possibly eat all of this."

"I wasn't sure what you liked." Joseph's smile returned. "Besides, you've lost weight since you came here. I want to make sure you have at least one good meal while I can."

At the bottom of the basket were plates and cutlery, and Joseph urged her to try a bit of everything. For a few minutes, they ate in silence, watching the sunlight sparkle on the dark lake. A fish, large and plump, breached the water and returned with a splash. Sophie looked at Joseph to see if he'd been watching it, but his eyes were on her. She looked back at her plate, both embarrassed and pleased.

"Would you tell me about the house?" she asked at last. "It must have an exceptional history."

"I'm not sure about exceptional so much as unusual," he replied, "but I'd be glad to tell you as much as I know. It was built a little over four hundred years ago by Matthias Argenton. Not much is known about him, except that he somehow came into a large sum of money very quickly and possibly wasn't as sound of mind as I would like to claim in an ancestor. He had Northwood constructed in this forest. At that time, it was even further from civilization than we currently are; the nearby town is only three hundred years old. Before then, it was nearly a full day's travel to the closest neighbor."

Sophie frowned. "What a strange thing to do."

"From all accounts, he was a strange person. The house was built to his exact specifications, which, as you can see, are nearly as eccentric as his choice of location."

The building's shadow stretched over the grass behind them. Even without looking at it, Sophie could picture the mammoth building, so large and complicated that she still couldn't find her way to her own bedroom.

"Did he have family?"

"Not at first, but he soon found that wealth could abolish a lot of faults in the eyes of a young woman. Matthias married within a year of Northwood's completion and had twelve children—all sons—over the following decade."

"Twelve sons," Sophie echoed in amazement. "It's a wonder they didn't consume his entire fortune."

Joseph chuckled. "Yes, indeed. But they thrived, and each brought their own brides back to Northwood, and the family quickly grew to more than fifty members. The following two centuries were Northwood's peak; the house was full and busy, there were more than enough staff to care for it, and, from what I gather, the family was all happy living together."

Sophie thought of the house's current residents: Joseph, Garrett, Rose, and Elise. It was a sad reduction for such a grand building.

"What happened?" she asked. "Did they move to the city or different parts of the country?"

"No." Joseph's face darkened a fraction. "If you're born at Northwood, there's a strong tendency to stay your whole life. I understand there was a disagreement between my grandparents and their siblings, which divided the house and caused many deaths."

The illustration of the wealthy woman decapitating her sister flashed before Sophie's eyes again. *The making of a vengeful ghost.* "What was the disagreement about?"

Joseph hesitated a fraction of a second too long for Sophie to believe his answer. "I'm not entirely sure, but I believe it was something petty."

She wanted to press him for the truth, but bit back on the impulse. They were finally talking; she didn't want to make him hostile again. "And so Northwood's occupants dwindled."

"Yes. While Matthias Argenton and his children all had large families, the trend reversed over the last few generations. Rose and Garrett have only one child; several of their aunts and uncles didn't have any."

"Would *you* like children?"

She'd said something wrong. Joseph's good humor disappeared abruptly, and the shutters returned to his eyes. "I did at one point, but I don't believe I do any longer."

Is that why he didn't come to me on our first night at Northwood? Does he intend to never *visit me?* It was a startling idea. Sophie had assumed she would be expected to give him heirs. The possibility of remaining childless had never occurred to her.

Sophie searched for something to undo her blunder. She loved the way Joseph smiled at her, and the return of his cool tone made her shrink a little on the inside. "I don't believe I thanked you for saving me last night."

If anything, that only increased his coldness. "Why would you thank me for allowing you to fall into such a horrific situation? If you're searching for a way to be kind to me, accepting my apology is, I suspect, more than I deserve."

This is so confusing. He clearly hates what happened last night... but he's not doing anything to prevent it occurring again. How can his loyalty to the house be that strong?

She'd hoped the picnic would be a chance for them to become closer, but it was turning sour, and Sophie had no idea how to reverse it. The panicky, choked feeling rose up to constrict her throat, and she pushed her half-eaten plate to one side.

"Sophie." The fingers that brushed her arm were almost as soft as his voice. "Forgive me. I didn't mean to spoil this morning for you. Come, I won't be angry any longer."

She tried to smile at him, but the emotions were too close to the surface to fight them back. Joseph's black eyes, full of mingled regret and affection, met hers for a moment, then he pulled her against him in a warm, enveloping embrace.

Sophie pressed her face to his jacket and inhaled deeply. He smelled good, like a forest after a heavy rain, mingled with spices and firewood. One hand wrapped around her back, and his other caressed her hair in slow, even strokes. She shivered at the touch.

"You're cold." He sighed and pulled back. The sudden lack

of contact left her with a heavy, empty feeling inside, but the deprivation was only temporary. Joseph shrugged off his jacket, wrapped it around her shoulders, then pulled her back into his arms.

They sat like that for a long while. Joseph stroked her hair, and she thought she felt him press a kiss to the top of her head. His heartbeat echoed in her ears. It was a good, strong tempo, and the anxiety in Sophie's chest ebbed as she nestled deeper into his arms.

"Why did you marry me?" she asked. Her voice was muffled in his shirt, though, and he had to pull back slightly.

"Pardon, my dear?"

"Why did you marry me?"

The smile was back, warming her insides. "I liked your hair."

Sophie laughed. "That's a terrible reason."

"It certainly is."

Her smile faltered. "Be honest with me. You're wealthy enough to recommend you to most of the city's available ladies. Why me? You hardly knew me."

He inhaled and let his breath out slowly. "That's true. I was in a bad situation when I met you that night at the opera. You looked—forgive me if this is too blunt—but you looked stunning. You were everything innocent and sweet and vulnerable. When I visited the following day, it was under the guise of a meeting with your father. But, truthfully, I was only there to see more of you. And when I heard what had happened to your father's shipment…"

He trailed off. Sophie finished the sentence for him. "You made an offer of marriage, knowing it wouldn't be refused."

Joseph sighed and squeezed her shoulders lightly. "I'm afraid so. Does that make me a terrible person? It was an impulse decision. But, my dear, you've done nothing but surprise me since."

Sophie desperately hoped she hadn't been a bad surprise. "How so?"

"I've already said my first impression was that you were sweet. That has been accurate, but I didn't expect you to have a sharp mind, as well." He nodded toward the bandage on his arm. "Or to care so deeply and show me so much kindness when you barely knew me."

Sophie buried her face against his chest so he couldn't see her embarrassment.

"I thought I was marrying a simple girl. But, somehow, I managed to find a woman I respect, whose company I enjoy more than I've enjoyed anything for a long time, and who I've learned to care for deeply." His voice was low and full of emotion. Sophie was gradually learning to identify his tones and realized, with a stab of surprise, that he was anxious. *He's afraid I'll reject him.*

She tilted her head up so that he could see her expression. She was so excited and nervous that she hardly knew what she was saying. "I—for you, too...so much..."

Surprise, then delight flooded his eyes, followed by something so deep and powerful that Sophie thought her heart might stop. "Sophie, my darling..."

He lowered his head toward her, slowly and cautiously, and Sophie closed her eyes.

She'd never imagined his lips could feel so good. They were firm, warm, and hesitant at first, but quickly became hungry as she returned the kiss. His hand tangled in her hair, pressing her against him. She wrapped her arms around his shoulders in return, and felt his muscles shift under her fingers. Her heart fluttered at the taste of his mouth, and when he finally pulled back, they were both breathing heavily. A smile spread over Joseph's face as his hands lingered on the back of her neck.

He loves me. The thought made her feel like her heart might explode. She'd never experienced so much happiness all at once before; she was shaking from it. *He actually loves me.*

"Sophie—" He wouldn't stop smiling, and in a moment, both of them were laughing. He kissed her cheeks, her forehead, her neck, and finally her lips again, and she responded by holding him as tightly as she dared.

They lay back on the picnic blanket, limbs tangled, simply enjoying the moment. Joseph's hand returned to stroking her hair and her neck, and Sophie kissed his fingers whenever they came close enough.

"I'd like to stay here forever," he said.

Sophie ran her hand over his sharp cheek and jaw, and felt a flutter of delight when he leaned into her touch. "We could. You brought enough food to last us for a few weeks at least."

He laughed. After a moment, he looked at the sky, though, and his expression sobered. "I would stay here with you all day and all night, if you would tolerate me for that long, but I'll need to leave quickly if I'm to return before dark."

Sophie felt like someone had doused her in icy water. "You're still going to town?"

"I'm afraid I must."

Sophie tilted her head back to look at Northwood. It loomed over her, patiently waiting for her to step through its doors and return to its vicious embrace. "Can I come with you?"

"Not this time, my darling. I'll be traveling by horseback to cover the road quickly." The frown returned as he examined her face. "Are you afraid?"

Yes. "I'll be fine."

He took her hand and kissed the back of each finger. "I'll return as quickly as I can. Stay in your room; you'll be safe there. And if you need help, ask Garrett. I know he seems indifferent, but he isn't. I've asked him to look out for you."

"Thank you."

"Would you like me to walk you to your room?"

The sun was still bright and high in the sky, and Sophie was reluctant to return to the house. "I'd like to stay outside a little longer, if that's all right."

He hesitated for a moment, and his eyes darted toward the woods. "That should be fine. But don't stray far from the house."

"Because of the wolves?"

"Yes."

It was another lie. That he was still keeping secrets cut Sophie deeply, but she tried to hide it with a smile.

He seemed on the verge of saying something more, but then apparently thought better of it and closed his mouth. The joy was gradually disappearing from his countenance as he surveyed the forest edge, and in a desperate bid to bring it back, Sophie ran her fingers over his jaw again. He smiled at her, but it was only a brief flicker of warmth. He sat up, and Sophie joined him, nestling close to his side. He wrapped his arm about her shoulders again and leaned his head on hers.

Ask him now. There's not going to be a better time.

"Joseph…" The words stuck in her throat. She'd been so certain of what she wanted before the picnic: to escape from Northwood, no matter the cost. But now, the cost—losing Joseph—was intolerable.

He spared her having to speak the words. "You want to leave. I know."

Be honest with him. He deserves it. "I want us to *both* leave. Together. We could stay at my father's, if accommodation is a problem. He wouldn't mind—"

Joseph kissed the top of her head. It was a sad, lingering gesture. Instead of responding to her request, he said, "I've made some terrible decisions."

Sophie waited for him to continue. She had the feeling that he was on the edge of sharing something monumental. Another fish leaped toward the sun, disturbing the lake's surface, but she barely noticed it.

"I'm doing all that's in my power to fix my mistakes, but…it will take time, and success is not guaranteed." The sadness in his voice was almost painful to hear.

"I'll help you," Sophie said, tightening her grip on his shirt. "Whatever it is, I'll help."

"How did I find a woman as good and sweet as you?" Joseph asked, kissing her hair again. "You put me to shame, Sophie, and shine a harsh light on all of my inadequacies."

"I-I didn't mean to."

He chuckled. "No, of course you didn't. Don't worry. I suspect it's good for me. It's growing late, though, and I've delayed my departure longer than I should have. I wish I could grant your request, but it's not in my power at this moment. However, my hope is that the worst of my transgressions will soon be healed, and then we can leave Northwood. But you must be patient, my darling, and trust me. I'm doing everything I can."

We can leave Northwood. They were the four words Sophie had desperately wanted to hear, and they lit a burning hope inside of her. "I can be patient. And I do trust you."

"Thank you, my darling." He slipped a hand under her chin, tilted her face toward his, then kissed her sweetly. He lingered before pulling away reluctantly, then he took back the jacket Sophie offered him and set out for the stables behind the house at a brisk walk.

CHAPTER 21
DRIFTING

AS JOSEPH DISAPPEARED FROM sight, Sophie pressed her fingers to her mouth. Her heart thundered as she struggled not to laugh from mingled shock and delight.

He really loves me.

She felt as though a storm had broken inside her chest. Her heart ached, but in a good, overfilled way. Her skin tingled where Joseph had touched it. She was already hungry for his return and for when she could hold him again, feel his arms about her, and hear his voice.

Joseph had never seemed so warm or vulnerable as he had that morning. She loved both his smiles and laugher and wanted to experience more of both. *It's almost like he's a different person outside of the house. Like its oppression lifts from him.*

Sophie turned back to the building. It stretched high above her, its turrets and buttresses seeming more *alive* than ever before. She couldn't shake the image of it being a hulking monster, crouched in the clearing as it waited for just the right moment to lunge and envelop its prey in its snapping jaw.

Movement caught her eye. One of the curtains on the second floor was fluttering back into place. Someone had been watching her, and Sophie knew who.

Rose. Does nothing escape her attention? Did she see me with Joseph? She'll be angry.

Fear nipped at her, threatening to strangle her new happiness. Sophie looked away from the house and saw a horse and rider coming around the side of the building. Joseph raised his hand in goodbye as he urged the horse into a gallop toward the path leading to Northwood's gate. Sophie returned the gesture. *Be safe and come back quickly,* she begged. *I don't know how long I can be here alone.*

She watched him until the gate had closed and his horse's flicking tail disappeared from view, then sighed. The picnic still lay on the cloth, but Sophie wasn't hungry. *I should pack it up and return it to the house so the staff can share it. But not just yet. I'll stay outdoors a little longer.*

Sophie piled the dishes back into the basket and wrapped the blanket about it so that it wouldn't be bothered by insects, then she stood and stretched.

The morning seemed to have melted away, and the sun had already passed its apex and was beginning its descent. Sophie followed the edge of the lake, pausing to catch glimpses of tiny fish darting through the weeds surrounding the shore. She heard a few quiet plops in the distance where the fish leaped out of the water.

When the lake began curving toward the forest, Sophie turned away and continued toward the back of the house. A garden, larger than she'd expected, had been carefully cultivated on a sunny rise. She walked among the beds to admire the vegetables and fruit trees. Beyond the gardens were the stables, where she could hear men working to clean the stalls. She didn't want to have to make small talk with strangers, so she backtracked toward the lake again.

The basket had been cleared away in the brief minutes she'd been behind the house, and a prickle of uneasiness crept up Sophie's back. *How closely were we being watched?*

She followed the lake's edge again, drawing closer to the forest than she would have dared if she hadn't felt the house's oppression so strongly. As she neared the clearing's edge, she was able to appreciate just how complex and dark the woods were. Some of the trees looked hundreds of years old; their great trunks stretched high above her. Between them was thick bracken, felled trees at various stages of decay, and long, strangling vines. *How does Joseph manage to walk through this? It looks like it would trip me every step I took.*

The groaning tree limbs and chattering animal noises were loud. Sophie thought she saw motion deep in the shadows, but it was too indistinct to make out. The forest seemed to mirror the house in its claustrophobic, dense nature. The wind was growing colder, and the hairs across the backs of Sophie's arms rose. She turned back to the lake and felt the breath seize up in her throat.

A body floated in the water. Its limbs had caught among the weeds near the shore, and its long black hair drifted in a thick cloud about its head.

Sophie pressed a hand to her mouth. Horror and revulsion strangled her voice. As the hair ebbed in the lake's gentle motion, Sophie caught a glimpse of the body's face. He must have been dead for a long time; the thick, leathery skin had puckered and bulged sickeningly. Its bleached lips were open, exposing rotten gums and dark, elongated teeth.

What should I do? Should I find someone in the house or wait for Joseph—

The corpse's eyes snapped open.

Sophie screamed and staggered away from the lake edge. The body's black, lifeless eyes followed her as she stumbled and fell to the ground. Then the creature began twisting, its decaying, atrophied limbs turning toward her.

Terror poured energy into Sophie's limbs. She regained her feet and ran for the house, clutching at her skirts so they wouldn't trip her again. She thought she heard a scraping, dragging noise following her, but she didn't dare turn to look as she reached the house. She threw herself up the stairs and wrenched open the door. After slipping through the gap, Sophie slammed the heavy barricade behind herself.

She leaned against the door, shivering and gasping, as tears blurred her eyes and her heart thundered. She remembered the figure she'd seen walking through the storm the morning before, and felt sick to her stomach. *Was it the same ghost or a new one?*

Either way, the spirits hadn't become dormant as Joseph had thought they would. And he was gone and wouldn't return for another six hours, and she had no idea what she was supposed to do without him.

A door creaked open behind her, and Sophie swiveled to face it. Garrett Argenton had come through the dining room and fallen still as he caught sight of her. If he was surprised to see her looking so disheveled or distressed, he didn't show it.

If you need help, ask Garrett, Joseph had said. Sophie hesitated, searching for a way to explain what had happened. *He must know about the spirits, too, surely? Has he seen them before?*

He clasped his hands behind his back as he waited for her to speak.

Sophie tried to wet her lips, but her tongue was too dry to do any good. "There was something…*alive*…in the lake."

Garrett gave a short nod. "I'll take care of it. Stay in your room."

Is it really that simple? He's just going to…take care of it?

"Be careful," Sophie said, hoping she wasn't speaking out of place.

Garrett's mustache twitched as he gave a barely audible snort. Sophie could feel his eyes on her back as she crossed to the stairs and climbed to the third floor. Her limbs were still shaking, but the image of the lake was starting to take on a numb, distant feeling, almost as though it had been an exceptionally unpleasant and vivid dream.

Sophie turned at the top of the stairs and saw Garrett was still by the door, watching her. *Why? To make sure I don't try to leave the house again?*

She rounded the corner to escape from the cold gaze then allowed herself to sink to the floor and rested her head on her knees. The nausea and shaking passed, but the dread didn't.

His eyes are just as cold as Joseph's used to be. What does he plan to do? Does he know a special way to fight or dispel the spirits? Surely not—if there was such a defense, Joseph would have told me about it. At least…I hope *he would have told me about it.*

Sophie moaned and pressed her palms against her temples. She'd felt so blissfully happy barely an hour before, when Joseph had held her close and kissed her hair. Just like the image of the lake's corpse, those feelings were starting to take on a dreamlike quality. *I told Joseph I would trust him. But is that wise? He's left me alone in a house with active spirits, and I don't even know why. What's so important in town that he had to travel there today?*

She lowered her hands to see the red-and-gold walls. The abhorrent, intricate pattern, a permanent reminder that she was living in a house of shadows and secrets, seemed to envelop her.

Everything seemed so simple when I was with Joseph. What wouldn't I give to wind back time and never let him go.

Her legs were steady, so Sophie got to her feet. She peeked around the corner to the stairwell into the foyer, but Garrett was no longer in view. *I didn't hear the door open. Did he go outside?*

Don't think about it. Sophie turned back to the hallway. *Not now, at least. Wait in your room. Joseph will be back in less than six hours. And when he is, he'll explain everything. He owes it to me.*

CHAPTER 22
ELISE

WHEN MARIE HAD SHOWN Sophie the way from her room to the stairwell that morning, Sophie had paid careful attention to the path. She retraced it then, mouthing the instructions to herself. *Right, second right, then left at the end of the hallway, and right again.*

She found herself in a hall that seemed familiar and followed it to the end. But when she turned the handle, she realized, with a horrible sinking feeling, that she was entering the wrong room. Her handle turned smoothly; this one squealed on its hinge. The door was already half-open before she realized her mistake, though, and Sophie stared at the room's interior in shock.

It was clearly lived in. The bed was neatly made with fresh sheets, and the curtains were pulled back to allow in the sickly afternoon light. The bureau's contents—ribbons, brushes, hair combs, and an expensive-looking doll—had been swept onto the floor.

They weren't the only things on the floor, though. Crude images had been drawn across the wooden boards with a charcoal pencil.

Against her better judgment, Sophie stepped into the room to gaze, horrified, at the pictures. The black Shadow Being loomed toward her a hundred times from the floor, and a hundred more stared from the walls. Every available surface had been drawn on. The sensation of so many pairs of empty white eyes fixed on her was overpowering.

Sophie covered her mouth to muffle her breathing. *This must be Elise's room. This is worse than I could have ever expected. How long did it take her to create this?*

She turned in a semicircle, captivated and horrified by the display. There was something almost familiar about the shadow figure, the way its limbs were extended unnaturally, and how its fingers were tipped with long, vicious claws. Sophie felt as though the pictures needed to be a little more detailed for her to make out the resemblance, but Elise's drawings were scrawled messily, almost frantically. The only clear parts were the lamp-like eyes.

An exhale behind her made Sophie gasp, and she swung around to find Elise standing in the doorway. The girl looked sick. Her face was white and sweaty, and the circles around her eyes were almost dark enough to look like stains. Her gaze was unfocussed, and Sophie wasn't entirely sure if Elise saw her.

I've seen that expression before. It was a stray dog that had been trapped. It was scared to the point of insanity; so frantic that it wasn't aware of its surroundings but deathly tired from its struggles.

Sophie felt tears build. What had Elise endured to gain that

145

look? She took a step toward the girl, half wanting to take her hands and promise help, and half wanting to simply hug her. But Elise spoke before Sophie could close the distance.

"Can't you hear him?" she asked. Her voice was as raw as it would have been if she'd spent the last hour screaming. "Can't you hear his whispers?"

"Elise, sweet, what's wrong?" Sophie took the girl's hands in hers. They were cold. She rubbed at them, trying to get warmth back into them.

Joseph, I'm sure you would have known what to do. Why did you have to leave me?

Elise exhaled, and her dazed eyes fixed on Sophie. "He wants you more," she said. "I'm sorry."

Who does she mean—Joseph or someone else? "Elise," Sophie said, fighting to keep her voice gentle and low, "has someone hurt you? Has your mother done something bad?"

"My mother?" A ghost of a smile spread across her pale lips. "Do you mean Rose? She can hear him, too, sometimes."

"Elise," Sophie started, but broke off as a silhouette appeared in the hallway behind the girl. Sophie let go of Elise's hands and straightened, feeling the blood drain from her face. Garrett had approached them so silently that she hadn't realized he was there until he was on top of them. His eyes roved across the drawings filling the room, but his face was expressionless; she couldn't tell if he was angry or simply surprised. He placed both hands on Elise's shoulders and moved her to one side so that she no longer blocked the doorway.

"Sir," Sophie began, lost for words.

Garret's voice was ice-cold. "Go back to your room."

She didn't dare disobey him and hurried past the pair, all but fleeing down the hallway. Just as she had in the foyer, she could feel Garret's eyes on her back the entire way.

She stumbled through the house's maze, trying to figure out where her carefully memorized pathway had led her wrong, but she was already aware that she'd become hopelessly lost during her flight from Elise's room. She took a hallway on a whim and, to her shock and immense relief, realized she recognized it. She opened the door at the end, entered her room, and sank onto her bed with a relieved gasp.

There's more wrong with this house than I ever could have imagined. What's happening to Elise? Why won't Joseph tell me? Is it because he knows I'll leave if I learn the truth? Should I leave?

She clenched her hands until they stopped shaking and squeezed her eyes closed until they dried. When she felt in control enough to stand, she went to the window and gazed at the bleak clearing.

Joseph gave me this room because it has the best view in the house. I think I would much rather not have a view at all.

The lake was still. That was a mercy. The trees rocked and shivered in the wind, and their groaning filled the room. Sophie fixed her eyes on the gate leading out of Northwood and didn't look away until she heard her door open some time later.

CHAPTER 23
MARIE

A FAMILIAR, SWEET FACE peeked around the door's edge, and Sophie felt a rush of relief. She held out her hand to her friend. "Marie! Come inside. I'm so glad to see you. I can't even begin to describe what's happened today—"

Sophie stopped short as she noticed how pale Marie's face seemed in the dim light and how shaky her smile was. *She's seen something.* "Come, sit on the edge of my bed. What's wrong? Has something happened?"

Marie nodded, and Sophie squeezed the girl's hand. "You can stay with me as long as you need to."

Marie clearly wanted to tell Sophie what she'd seen, but Sophie couldn't understand the wild gestures. Marie mimed writing on her hand, and Sophie fetched sheets of paper, the pen, and the ink well from her table and propped them on the bed between them. "Can you write?"

Marie shook her head, took up the pen, and began drawing on the paper. Sophie leaned closer and tried to guess what the images meant.

First Marie drew a house with tall turrets. That was easy. "Northwood."

Marie nodded and drew a crude face with a finger pressed over its lips.

"Secrets?"

She nodded again.

The next image was harder to guess. It wasn't until Marie scrawled over the figure's dress multiple times, making it bigger and fancier with each pass, that it clicked for Sophie. "Woman. A wealthy lady. Ah—of course—Rose."

Marie drew a large cross beside the woman.

Sophie felt a crawling sensation rise in her stomach. "You don't like her."

The maid nodded, but she wasn't finished. She pointed to Sophie, then to Rose, then to the cross.

"You think I should stay away from her?"

More nodding followed, and the gestures were repeated, but in reverse.

"*She* doesn't like *me*."

Sophie had found the crux of the message, and Marie pressed her hand to reinforce the message. Sophie tried to smile, but it felt more like a grimace. "Thank you for warning me. I'll be careful."

Marie discarded the page and began drawing again. Her face had darkened.

Sophie watched a tall rectangle appear on the paper, with a squiggly shape halfway down. "A door."

A wave of Marie's hand told Sophie to keep guessing.

"Is it the front door? You think I should leave?"

A vague gesture suggested Marie didn't disagree, but it wasn't the image's intended meaning. She scrawled around the door's frame several times, but Sophie's guesses were becoming more erratic, and Marie scowled in frustration. She dropped the pen, raised her thumb to her mouth, and bit it hard.

"Marie," Sophie gasped, but the girl brought her thumb back to the page before Sophie could stop her.

A bead of blood had appeared where she'd pierced her skin, and Marie smeared it across the image of the door.

Sophie stared at the red mark and swallowed. "The red door."

Vigorous nodding affirmed the guess. Marie moved the picture to one side and began drawing again, this time more slowly and carefully.

Sophie couldn't bring herself to look at the new image. The panic was back in full force, and it was all she could do to keep her voice steady. "Marie, did you open the door?"

At Marie's nod, Sophie felt her heart plunge. "Marie, you shouldn't have. Joseph—Mr. Argenton—says it's not safe."

Marie nodded again, her eyes large.

Sophie thought back to that morning, when Marie had tried to tell her something as they'd left her room. *She had a plan—was this it? Did she explore the house…for me?*

The girl's loyalty was overwhelming, but at the same time, it terrified Sophie. *This isn't the sort of house that lets you uncover its secrets without consequences. What if she'd been hurt? She was there on my behalf—how could I forgive myself if she'd come to harm?*

Marie finished her drawing. She pointed to the page with the blood-dyed door then pointed to her new image, which she held up for Sophie to see.

"Sweet mercy…"

It was the shadow monster, looming out of inky blackness, its empty white eyes boring into Sophie's soul.

Feeling faint, she pressed a hand to her mouth as a rushing noise filled her ears. Marie discarded both pages quickly and gripped Sophie's shoulder to prop her upright.

It's almost identical to what Elise has been drawing. Did Marie see those pictures? Or is this her own experience?

Sophie took her hand away from her mouth. "Marie, is that what you saw when you opened the door?"

One look at the girl's haunted eyes answered the question even before Marie nodded.

"You mustn't ever go back there again. Mr. Argenton says we may be able to leave Northwood soon. But it's dangerous as long as we stay here. Don't go searching for these sorts of things."

Marie nodded, resolute, and squeezed Sophie's hand again. Sophie smiled at her and squeezed back. "Thank you, Marie. I wouldn't wish this house on anyone, but I'm grateful I have you with me."

The door creaked on its hinges, and both Sophie and Marie started. Rose, resplendent in a forest-green dress, stood in the doorway, hands folded neatly in front of her. Her dead eyes flickered across the drawings scattered over Sophie's bed and lingered over the page with the Shadow Being. Sophie thought Rose's eyebrows rose a fraction, then she fixed her gaze on Marie.

"I need your assistance." Her voice was empty of emotion but not unkind. "Please come with me, Marie."

Both Sophie and Marie stood up. Sophie dreaded what Rose might say about her conduct with Joseph, but the older woman turned and left the room without even glancing at her. Marie gave a brief smile, which Sophie returned, then the maid hurried from the room to catch up to her employer. Sophie waited until both sets of footsteps faded from her hearing before allowing herself to breathe again.

She was certain Rose had seen her at the lake that morning, and Sophie had expected her next encounter with the woman to bring a fresh and cruel punishment. But Rose hadn't spoken to her. She hadn't even looked at her. It was as if Sophie hadn't been in the room. *Maybe that's her retaliation—to ignore me. I wouldn't be upset if it were.*

Too anxious to keep still, Sophie picked the drying pictures off her bed and looked at them. Marie believed she should be careful around Rose. All of Rose's hostilities had occurred when they were alone together, though, so what had Marie seen or heard to bring about her opinion?

Sophie flipped through to the final page. The black creature, though drawn quickly, was still more detailed than it had been in Elise's pictures. She could make out the sharp fangs that filled its dark maw. The claws, extending in long arcs from its knuckles, nearly scraped the floor. The white circles of its eyes were large and perfectly round. *Intent. Hungry.*

Sophie folded the paper and tucked it inside her dress. She could show it to Joseph when he returned. He'd told her that Elise had read about the monster in a book, but Marie's experience brought the lie into sharp relief.

She hoped Marie would come back when Rose no longer needed her. Sophie had a lot of questions and thought Marie could use drawings to communicate the answers. Even if she couldn't, it would be nice to talk with someone who hadn't spent her whole life in Northwood.

Sophie frowned as a new thought hit her. She'd been so shocked by Rose's appearance that she hadn't even considered what task her aunt wanted Marie for that one of the other maids couldn't help with.

No... Sophie started upright. Anger at her own stupidity rushed through her, closely followed by cold, sickening dread.

Why didn't I realize it before? If Rose wished to truly, deeply hurt me, she'd be too smart to attack me directly. She'd go after someone more vulnerable. Someone I cared about... She'd hurt Marie in my place.

Sophie ran from her room, but Rose and Marie had long disappeared. She stopped where the pathways split, trying to guess which direction they'd taken.

"Marie?" Her voice echoed through the passageways, bouncing back at her from a dozen different directions. Sophie wrung her hands then turned toward the main stairwell. "Marie! Can you hear me?"

She knew the house was too vast for there to be any chance of finding them quickly, but she still had to try. Panic nipped at her heels as she rushed through the twisting passageways. The staircase loomed ahead. *Would Rose have stayed on this level or gone up or down?* Sophie hesitated, one hand on the balustrade, aware that every second she wasted might have dire consequences.

Make a choice!

She went downstairs first, hoping Rose might have gone to the kitchens or the dining room. Her footfalls were a loud drum as she leaped down the stairs and crossed the foyer.

A door to her left stood open, and Sophie went to it. She recognized the gun storage room where she'd found the butler the day before. The shelves each held a gun, cleaned and lined up neatly, save for one.

The cold dread in Sophie's chest plunged its fangs into her heart. She turned back to the stairs in a flurry, screaming, "Marie! Marie!"

A single gunshot rang through the building. The crack seemed to shake the walls and lingered in Sophie's ears.

"No! Marie, no!" Sophie took the stairs three at a time, stumbling and scrambling in her desperation to follow the noise. It led her back to the third floor, where she turned left. From there she was lost; she took the twists quickly, glancing into every open door and turnoff she passed, trying to following the echoes she imagined still rang in her ears. "Marie! Can you hear me? Marie!"

Sophie turned a corner and pulled up short. Rose stood in her path, hands neatly clasped at her front and a broad smile parting her red-dyed lips. It was almost identical to the expression she'd worn on the day she'd greeted Sophie.

"Well, my dear." Rose's voice was a calm and deadly purr. "Perhaps now you'll reconsider before trying to twist my nephew from his duty."

Sophie's gaze dropped to Rose's dress. The forest-green garment was perfectly tailored and impeccably crafted. Its high neckline brushed Rose's jaw, and its ruffles would have done a queen credit. A spray of dark-red liquid stained the bodice.

"Where's Marie?" The words came out as a terrified croak.

Rose's smile widened, and she stretched one graceful hand out to indicate to the offshoot she stood next to. As she raised her arm, three men came out from the hallway: the butler and two footmen. They were all deathly pale, and one of the footmen was sweating so profusely, it stained his shirt. They dropped their eyes as they passed Sophie, seemingly determined not to look at her.

Rose still stood at the hallway's entrance, her smile and outstretched arm a cruel invitation. Sophie moved as though she were in a dream. The air felt thick; it stuck in her throat and burned her lungs. Repulsed chills crawled across her back as she drew nearer to Rose. She didn't dare break eye contact until she'd reached the hallway, then she turned to look down it.

The wallpaper changed to black and gold. In the distance—it seemed very far away—the red door stretched nearly to the ceiling. At its foot lay what looked like a bundle of white cloth.

Sophie caught sight of a limp hand extending from the heap, and a strangled scream rose into her throat. She ran toward the figure, already dreading what she was about to see.

Marie lay at the door's foot, wrapped in a large cloth. Sophie dropped to her knees and tugged the fabric away from her friend. Marie's sightless eyes gazed at the ceiling, unfocussed in death.

"No, no, no, please—"

Sophie caressed the girl's face, trying to wake her, but Marie's body was already beginning to cool.

"*Marie!*" The word rose into a scream, and once she'd started, Sophie couldn't stop. She shrieked, shaking Marie's body as hot, furious tears spilled from her.

This is your fault, a cold little voice whispered to her. *Marie is dead because of you.*

Large hands gripped Sophie's shoulders and began pulling her back. She struggled, but they wouldn't let her go. She twisted and, through the tears blinding her, saw Garrett Argenton was dragging her away from the body.

"Don't touch me. Don't touch me!" she cried, clawing at his hands.

He grunted as her nails cut him, but he didn't let go. "There's nothing you can do for her now," he said. "Come away."

The words filled her head. *Nothing you can do now. But you could have stopped this. If you'd been a little quicker, a little smarter, you would have realized what Rose was planning. You could have stopped her…barricaded the door…protected Marie. But you allowed her to be a target then failed to save her when she was in danger.*

Sophie wailed in shame and horror, then slumped, too exhausted to struggle anymore. She couldn't stop sobbing and couldn't draw breath fast enough to fuel her limbs. Garrett wrapped an arm around her and dragged her down the hallway, only stopping when they reached its end, where Rose waited for them. He let Sophie collapse to the floor then straightened to face the tall woman. "Why are you doing this?"

"Our nephew has forgotten his purpose." Rose's smile had died into a sneer. "Have you seen Elise today? It hasn't let her alone. She's *dying*, and yet Joseph still tries to protect this girl."

"He says he has a hope of banishing it completely."

"Ha! You know as well as I do that it's a fool's errand. Have you forgotten how many of our forebears held similar hopes? Their blood has *painted* this house. He should know better, especially after what happened to his mother—"

Garrett turned away with a hiss.

Rose crossed her arms, her eyes glittering. "We can't indulge our nephew any further. If he won't do it, we must take the task upon ourselves."

Garret's dark eyes flicked to Sophie, then he looked away, as though he were ashamed to meet her gaze. "I promised Joseph we would wait a full day. If it's in vain—"

"It will be. And while you wait, your own daughter is dying. Is that what you want?"

The lines about Garrett's face hardened as his voice dropped to a bitter murmur. "Sometimes I wonder if it wouldn't be kinder."

A door slammed, and the three of them jumped. Sophie,

whose tears had reduced to a terrified trickle, scrambled toward the hallway. "Marie!"

What she saw sent ice through her veins. The hallway was empty. Someone—or something—had taken Marie's body through the red door.

Garrett placed a heavy hand on her shoulder, but Sophie slapped it away. She staggered to her feet and leaned against the wall to keep herself steady. "What have you done with her?"

Garrett didn't answer, but Rose stepped forward, her red-lipped smile stretching wide. "Why don't you see for yourself?"

Sophie faced the hallway. The red door called to her; she was aware of the whispery noises, far louder than they'd ever been before, but still too quiet to make out the words over her thundering heart.

Rose placed a cold hand on Sophie's arm. "You can still catch her if you're quick."

Sophie shook the hand off and backed away from the pair. She didn't dare take her eyes off them until she'd reached the main hallway, then she turned and ran.

I'm so sorry, Marie. Fresh tears ran down her face. Her eyelids were sore and swollen, and the ache in her chest was more severe than anything she'd felt before. *I'm sorry I couldn't protect you, after everything you did for me. You didn't deserve this.*

She couldn't count the number of times she'd become lost on Northwood's third floor, but that day, whether by pure luck or because the house had decided she'd endured enough, she found her room almost immediately. She slipped through the door, locked it behind herself, then pressed her palms against her eyes as she tried to smother her grief-filled wails.

It's time to leave.

CHAPTER 24
THE FOREST

SOPHIE FOUND HER TRAVEL cases stored neatly in the cupboard. She took out the largest one, opened it on the bed, then began throwing anything she might need inside: her brushes and reticule went in first, followed by any jewelry she thought she would be able to sell. Then she wrenched open the wardrobe doors and began taking out the dresses—the horrible, sickening dresses Rose had chosen for her—and bundling them into the case.

She hated herself for not realizing that Marie had been in danger. She hated Rose for everything the woman had done and intended to do. And she hated Joseph for his lies and concealments and for abandoning her at Northwood…but she didn't hate him as much as she wanted to.

Her head warned her that he would turn out to be as twisted as his toxic family, and she had to leave him forever if she wanted to be safe. But her aching heart screamed at the idea. *I must see him again.* If nothing else, she was sure he'd been genuine during their morning by the lake, when he'd stroked her hair and smiled at her so warmly. In that moment, she'd felt as if she had a chance to be happy.

It only took her a moment to make up her mind. She would leave Northwood immediately and wait outside the gate for Joseph's return. There, she would give him an ultimatum. He could come away with her, and they could start a new life together, or they could part at the gate and never see one another again. Under no circumstances would she step back inside Northwood's bounds—not even if he tried to carry her in.

Sophie turned back to the wardrobe and reached for another armful of dresses. There was something strange about them, though—something Sophie couldn't immediately make sense of. The gauzy garments bulged outward, as though a large shape hid behind them. She stared at them in confusion. *They didn't look like that a moment ago.*

Then a sound reached her—a very low, very quiet exhale. The noise seemed to pass through Sophie, rattling her core. She reached a shaking hand toward the dresses, unable to stop herself, and tugged the closest one aside.

An ash-white face stared at her through the gap. Sophie shrieked and scrambled away. Her back bumped into her bed as she pressed her hands over her heart.

The dresses bulged forward and parted as the specter behind them stepped out of its confinement. One bare foot hit the floor with a muted thud then was followed by the other.

Sophie stared at the figure's face, unable to believe what she was seeing. The skin was white enough to have been a bleached tablecloth, and the eyes were stained entirely black. The lips, so awfully familiar, held a ghastly blue-green tint. Unruly in life, her hair now hung like a limp curtain around her face. The face, despite the contortions of death, was sickeningly familiar.

"Marie," Sophie breathed.

Marie's lips parted. Inside her mouth was black and filled with small, angular teeth. The sightless eyes fixed on Sophie, and Marie lurched forward, her bony fingers reaching toward Sophie's face.

Sophie threw herself toward the door. She seized the cold metal handle and pulled, but it wouldn't budge. Marie inhaled, making a sickening rattle, as though it had come from a woman on her deathbed. Then there was a footstep, ponderously heavy, as the dead girl moved nearer.

You fastened the door's lock when you came in. Unlock it!

Sophie tugged at the dead bolt. It stuck in its bracket and groaned in protest as she tried to drag it free. Marie took another step closer, halving the distance between them, her raspy breathing filling Sophie's ears. She couldn't think; her whole awareness had become condensed to the space behind her, where the spirit drew closer, its hands stretched toward her exposed back. Then the bolt pulled free, and Sophie yanked open the door just as Marie's fingers grazed her neck.

A strangled cry escaped Sophie as she tumbled into the hallway. The ghost's fingers had felt like ice on her skin. She didn't stop to see if Marie was following her before she snatched up her skirts and fled.

Sophie wove through the house's maze so quickly that her shoulders bumped the corners. She found her way to the stairs without passing another soul and took them to the ground floor at a reckless speed.

The butler stood by the gun storage room. He calmly watched Sophie as she dashed past but made no move to stop her.

Sophie tore open the door. The sun was setting, and it cast a sickly red glow across the washed-out landscape. Sophie was breathless and gasping, but she didn't let herself slow down as she took the steps to the lawn and followed the dirt path to Northwood's gates.

She wanted to cry, but she had no tears left in her body. Her eyes ached, her lungs burned, and she felt as though she might be sick. Once again, the black-and-white drawing appeared in her mind. *The making of a vengeful ghost.* As if Marie's untimely death hadn't been cruel enough, was she also cursed to linger in Northwood instead of finding rest in the next life?

The sun had dipped behind the treetops. Although it still spread its red glow over the sky, the clearing was shrouded in heavy shadow. Sophie felt too bone-weary to run any longer and settled for a fast walk as she climbed the hill toward Northwood's exit.

She'd left her travel case in her room, but nothing could entice her to return for it. *I don't care where I end up or what happens. As long as I don't starve and never have to return to Northwood, I'll consider myself the luckiest woman in the world.*

The gate loomed ahead, its black wrought iron the only thing standing between her and freedom. Sophie gripped the metal bars and pulled, but the gate stuck. She dug her feet into the ground and tugged harder, then she tried pushing and finally searched for some type of bolt or seal, without any luck.

They can't be stuck; Joseph went through them just this afternoon. She strained against the gate until her arms ached, then she staggered away, panting.

The house doesn't want me to leave. The thought was accompanied by a sinking, sickening feeling in her stomach. *Just like Joseph, it wants to keep me here forever.*

She glanced at the house. Lights were appearing in its windows as the staff, many probably still ignorant that their mistress had left, tried to chase away the darkness.

I have to find a way out.

A stone wall extended from either side of the gate and disappeared into the trees. Though too high to climb, it still gave Sophie a glimmer of hope. *It can't wrap around the entire clearing; it looks like it might only go on for a dozen meters before ending. I could walk around it then follow it back to the road.*

That meant going through the forest, though. The tangle of dark trees sent prickles up Sophie's arms. Still, she approached it. She followed the curve of the clearing a little way then turned and pressed into Northwood Forest's smothering depths.

Branches scratched at her exposed arms and snagged her hair as Sophie ducked and wove through the trees. She hadn't realized how unstable the ground would be; decades of partially decayed leaves and sticks crumbled under every footfall, threatening to collapse entirely. Sophie clung to the branches when she could, ignoring the stinging of her scraped hands as she searched for the stone wall.

It can't be far away, surely.

She could barely see in the clustered, dim woods. Every time she raised her eyes, she hoped to catch a glimpse of the gray stones through the trees, but all she could make out were shadows.

Maybe I'm past the wall's end already. Should I turn and try to find the road? Or should I go forward for a little longer?

Sophie paused, breathing heavily, as she tried to orient herself. Hidden beneath the cacophony of rubbing branches and wild animal calls, Sophie thought she could make out another, less natural noise. It sounded like whispers spoken through dry lips, punctuated by clicking teeth. Sophie, one hand gripping a thick branch that extended above her head, rotated on the spot, trying to make out shapes in the dying light. She thought there was some movement to her right, but whether it was from nature or something more sinister, she couldn't tell.

Her nerves were frayed to the edges of their endurance, but she pressed forward, trying to guess the direction of the road. It was far too easy to become disoriented in the woods; she couldn't be certain which direction she faced any longer.

The whispering noises grew louder, rising over the forest's sounds. Sophie kept her eyes moving, alternating watching where she was about to step and scanning her surroundings. Laughter rang out in the distance. It was cold and mirthless, a sickening debasement of the true emotion that should accompany laughter. Sophie moved faster, using her arms as much as her legs to clamber through the vegetation while cold sweat coated her and stuck her hair to her face.

Her dress became snagged, and she twisted to pull it free. A sharp tug couldn't dislodge it, though, and Sophie leaned closer to see what she'd become caught on. She gasped.

Bone-thin, blackened fingers gripped the edge of her skirt. She could see the knuckles bulging against the papery skin. She followed the arm across the leaf-strewn forest floor then raised her eyes to see the distorted, skull-like face leering at her.

CHAPTER 25
JOSEPH

JOSEPH COULDN'T KEEP HIMSELF from scanning Northwood's visage as he approached the building. On nights like that one, when the sunset painted the skies in reds and golds, Northwood almost looked romantic. His mouth twisted at the idea.

Sophie's window overlooked the house's entrance. He wondered if she was waiting for him, as she had been that morning. The curtains were open, but he saw no movement inside.

A single apprehension had been playing through his mind like a mantra since he'd left her that morning. *What if something happens while I'm gone? What if she's hurt?*

The thought sickened him. He'd urged his horse as fast as he dared on the journey, but it had still taken him six hours to return—six hours, and all for a fool's errand.

The bitter, painful failure left him with an impossible choice. He'd second-guessed himself more during the previous two days than he had at any other point in his life. *Maybe I should have told her about the house, after all. She deserves to know the truth.*

He'd been on the verge of telling her that morning, but he'd convinced himself that it would be better for her if he delayed the painful moment. There had been a chance to fix the situation and ensure Sophie's safety without her ever having to know the house's history—but any hope of that had been dashed by the sight that had greeted him in the inn's small, musty room.

He expected Sophie to hate him when she found out why he'd brought her to Northwood. In the meantime, he'd clung to the small moments of delight like a drowning man. Her fingers, tiny and delicate, bandaging his arm. Her silky skin and impossibly soft hair. The way she dropped her eyes when she was embarrassed. She made him feel alive like nothing else could, and the idea of losing her was a living nightmare.

He pushed through Northwood's doors and inhaled the familiar, cold air. Even after a lifetime of enduring it, the smell still managed to turn his stomach.

Reynolds, the butler, stood by to take his coat, but Joseph didn't stop. He had to see Sophie and reassure himself that she was safe. Everything else could wait until after.

The house seemed unnaturally quiet as he jogged up the stairs and turned toward Sophie's room. The maids were hiding again, and the implications of that sent chills up his spine.

Please let her be safe. She's already endured so much. If she's seen something—if the house has done anything…

He knocked on her door and, when there was no answer,

pushed into her room. It was empty. An open case lay on the bed, abandoned halfway through being filled. Joseph's mouth dried. He scanned the room and saw no signs of a struggle, although some of her dresses had been dropped onto the floor.

Rose had come up behind him while he was distracted. She moved so silently those days, he had no idea how she managed it. He wouldn't have known she was there except for her quiet, delighted exhale.

He turned toward her, and one look at her face told him she knew something. She bared her teeth in a smile. The insanity that had been creeping into her eyes over the past four months seemed more pronounced than ever. Joseph tried to keep his voice calm, despite the fear shredding his insides. "Where's Sophie?"

"Gone," Rose murmured. She crossed her arms over her chest like a hug and inhaled deeply. "Finally gone."

Joseph had to clench his fists to stop himself from shaking his aunt. He had no hope of hiding the panic in his voice this time. "Where is she? I swear, if you've hurt her—"

"Ha! No, no, no." Rose was delighted. She swayed as she tightened her arms about herself. "I haven't spilled so much as a single drop of her blood, my dear. She's managed that all by herself."

CHAPTER 26
THE DEAD

SOPHIE SCREAMED AS THE corpse latched a second hand onto her dress and began to drag itself toward her. She'd never imagined something so nightmarish could exist; its skin had dried into a thick leather over its sunken cheeks. Its eye sockets were empty, but its head bobbed as though it were still trying to see her. Patches of sparse black hair sprouted from its skull and fell past its shoulders. Any flesh under the skin had melted away over the years, leaving nothing to cushion the sharp angles of its bones. It opened its mouth to expose rows of small, sharply pointed teeth, and a rasping gurgle escaped its throat.

Sophie shrieked and kicked at the hands pinning her in place. Her foot smashed through one of them. The bones splintered under the impact, and the sensation made her stomach revolt. She gave her skirts another hard tug and managed to snatch them free from the second hand.

She didn't spare even a second to gather herself before running, tearing through the forest without regard for the hard branches that scratched her face and limbs. She'd taken only three paces when her foot plunged into a hole hidden by the forest's debris. Sharp pain shot through her ankle, and Sophie smothered a cry.

She grabbed a nearby tree trunk, digging her fingernails into the bark to drag herself free from the hole. Her foot ached. There was no time to check if it could still take her weight; she began running again, biting back against the stabbing pain that accompanied each step.

There was movement all around her. Shapes materialized from between the trees and rose from under the forest's litter. Bony hands reached toward her, and Sophie ducked and wove as well as she could in the forest's cramped confines.

Dead fingers caught in her hair and pulled her back. Pain shot across her skull, and she fell, slamming into a fallen tree trunk with a heavy thud. She rolled over and found herself face-to-face with one of the corpses. Its skin had split and bubbled, leaving dark cracks across its face. Sophie thrashed to pull herself free, but more hands fixed over her limbs and tangled in her hair. Then blinding, hot pain shot through her arm as one of the corpses bit into her flesh.

A crack deafened Sophie, and the pain in her arm ebbed to a dull sting as the creature released her. After a second crack, dark fragments sprayed over her. She blinked at them, dazed, and saw that what looked like bone fragments had fallen over her dress.

"Sophie, keep your head down!"

The voice, beautifully familiar, filled Sophie with burning relief. She ducked her head as instructed, and another crack released the pressure on her hair. The air filled with a horrible, furious hissing as the dead surrounding her reacted to their attacker.

She raised her head just enough to see Joseph racing through the trees. He paused, raised the gun to his eye, and fired. The bullet shattered one of the corpse's skulls, spraying Sophie with more bone chips while freeing her arms. She raised them over her head to protect herself and felt hot blood dripping from her elbow.

Joseph was almost on top of them. He turned the gun around and used its butt to smash one of the creatures away from her. More corpses were materializing out from the trees, converging on Joseph and snatching at his legs. He fought furiously, using the gun and his fists to shatter the desiccated bodies, pausing only to crush any grasping hands that came too close to Sophie.

The first time she'd met Joseph, Sophie had imagined his cool exterior hid something as dangerous as a wolf. She hadn't been wrong. Her husband's face was contorted into an animalistic snarl as he fought for her, and his eyes blazed with a dark, dangerous fury. He had no reservations in the fight and attacked mercilessly, beating back the corpses until she was surrounded by nothing but a scattering of broken limbs and crushed skulls.

Joseph stood for a moment, breathing heavily as he glanced around them to search for any further assailants. Then he discarded the gun and dropped to his knees beside Sophie, and all of the ferocity melted into fear and grief.

"My darling—" He caught sight of her bleeding arm and groaned. "Forgive me, Sophie. Shh, you're safe now. Come, let me…" He wrapped his arms around Sophie and picked her up with slow, deliberate care.

She pressed her face to his chest. His heart beat quickly in her ear, and she closed her eyes to soak in the sound. The entirety of the events from the afternoon washed through her. Grief, pain, and overwhelming fear collided, dulling her mind and making her limp in Joseph's arms. She was aware of movement but couldn't imagine what he was doing or where he was taking her. Joseph spoke to her in quiet, calm tones, but she couldn't make out the words. Then cold light spread over them, and Sophie opened her eyes to see they had escaped from the smothering forest and were standing in natural moonlight.

"Stay with me just a little longer," Joseph said. "We'll be inside soon."

"No." Sophie finally began to struggle. "No, I'm not going back. Not to Northwood."

"Calm down, Sophie. We have to. Please stop fighting—we don't have a choice."

"Let me go," Sophie spat, shoving against Joseph's chest. Her energy had been drained, and she couldn't pull free, but her exertion was enough to make Joseph kneel on the grass so that he wasn't in danger of dropping her. He wrapped his arms about her and held her still against his chest until her struggles died. Sophie fought to breathe properly. Still, she managed to put force into her words. "I'm not going back to Northwood."

"You're in shock. And you're injured. I need to get you medical attention, or you might not survive the night."

"I'd prefer death than that house."

Joseph sighed and buried his face into her hair.

She realized he was shaking. *What from? Fear?*

"Sophie, if there was any way for us to leave Northwood, I would take you away this very second. But we have no choice. I'm so sorry."

Sophie scowled. "What are you saying? Of course we can leave Northwood. I don't mind walking, but we can take the carriage if you prefer."

"*Don't mind walking…*" Joseph chuckled, but the sound died almost immediately. He stroked a hand through her hair as he sighed. "It's not as simple as that. If we try to leave, Northwood will kill us."

Sophie didn't speak for a moment. The numb sensation was starting to fade, and the pain was returning. She examined Joseph's face. It was pale and anxious, and there was a terrible resignation about his eyes. *Northwood will kill us.* She understood the words, but they made no sense. "No more secrets," she said at last. "You've been lying to me ever since I came here. If you want me to trust you, you have to tell me everything."

"I will," he said. "It's been long overdue, my darling. Forgive me; I won't conceal the matter any longer. But first, I need to get you inside. You're half-frozen and bleeding."

Without replying, Sophie nestled her head against Joseph's shoulder. He took that as a silent acceptance, lifted her, and resumed the long walk back to the house.

Neither of them spoke as they passed through Northwood's doors and crossed the silent foyer. Joseph carried her to the third floor and navigated the now-familiar hallways that led to her bedroom.

"Not my room," Sophie said. The memory of Marie, her face distorted in death, flashed across her eyes. She squeezed them closed so that she wouldn't have to see it again.

"Will mine be all right?"

She gave a short nod, and Joseph brought her to the bedroom she'd seen on her first night at Northwood. It was just as clean and orderly as she remembered it. A fire had been lit, and it cut through the chill.

Joseph carefully lowered her into the stuffed armchair in front of his fire. He left her for a moment, but when he returned, he was bearing thick blankets, which he wrapped around her.

"Tell me about the house," Sophie said.

"In a moment. Let me clean your wound first." Joseph pulled the rope that would summon the staff. Someone knocked at the door almost immediately, and Joseph spoke to the maid. Sophie couldn't make out his words, but his tone was brusque. She took advantage of Joseph's distraction and pulled the blanket away from her arm to check the cuts. The corpse's teeth had created two semicircles of punctures a few inches below her shoulder. The bleeding had stopped, but her arm was coated in gore.

She covered the wound again when she heard the door close. Joseph pulled the second seat nearer and sat on its edge, his dark eyes scanning her face.

Sophie felt as though she might explode from the questions and thoughts swimming through her mind. She was becoming more aware as the shock wore off and the fire warmed her, but she still struggled to put her thoughts into words.

"Would you like some laudanum for the pain?" Joseph asked.

Sophie shook her head. "It stops me from thinking clearly."

"You don't have to tell me what happened if you'd prefer not to." Joseph's face was darker than she'd ever seen it, focused and intense. "It would allow me to help you more if I knew, though."

Sophie turned to look through the window. The moon, large and bright, cast blue highlights over the treetops. "Rose killed Marie."

Joseph exhaled and pressed his fingertips against the bridge of his nose. He didn't speak, but Sophie could sense his pain.

"They left her body outside of the red door. Then…she *came back*." Sophie pulled the blankets around herself more tightly. "She wasn't a ghost. Neither were those things in the forest. They weren't alive, but they weren't spirits, either."

"No, they're not." The words were a low, defeated murmur.

"And the red door hides more than disrepair, doesn't it?"

"Yes."

After a knock at the door, Joseph rose to answer it then brought back an armful of supplies. He left towels and hot water at the foot of her chair then returned to retrieve a tray of tea and a plate of cookies.

"Eat. They will give you strength." He placed the cookies on the table beside Sophie. Sitting on the edge of his chair, he nodded at Sophie's arm. "May I?"

"Only if you tell me what you meant when you said Northwood would kill us."

A faint smile lit up his face. "You're tenacious. But yes, I promised I would explain. And I will. I won't keep a single thing from you, no matter how unpleasant it may be to both of us. You deserve to know everything."

Sophie nodded and picked up the cup of tea. Her hands were shaking and threatened to spill it, so she placed it back on the table and took up a cookie instead.

Joseph tugged the corner of the blanket away, and his eyebrows contracted. "Forgive me. I could have prevented this if I'd been faster."

It could have been a lot worse, too, Sophie thought, but she didn't say anything. She knew she had to keep her guard up against Joseph, no matter how good it felt to have his fingers brush over her arm and squeeze her hand. She had to stand her ground.

Joseph dampened the cloth and began to dab the blood away from the cuts. It was almost a perfect replica of the morning he'd come home with scratches over his arms, but instead of doing the tending, Sophie was being tended to. The intensity in his eyes worried her so much that she turned back to watch the fire. Sensing that Joseph was gathering his thoughts, she ate the cookie in silence while she waited.

"I don't expect you to forgive me for what I've done," he said at last, throwing away the dirty towel to pick up a fresh one. "All I ask is that you'll trust my intentions are now good, and allow me to help you as much as is in my power."

Sophie stayed silent.

"I'll tell you it all in the most logical order I can. It all begins with the house's creation, four hundred years ago."

CHAPTER 27
SECRETS

JOSEPH FOCUSED ON CLEANING and dressing Sophie's wounds as he spoke. His voice was subdued, and he seemed almost ashamed to meet her eyes. Sophie listened in silence, except for a few brief questions. The story was fantastical to the point of being absurd, but she couldn't disregard it. She trusted the speaker, and what he told her dovetailed with her own experiences.

"I tried to be truthful when I explained the house's history this morning," Joseph said. "But I didn't tell you everything. Matthias Argenton, the man who built Northwood, was a noble who had lost his title and land. He was an outcast, disgraced and penniless. From what I can gather, he spent many years traveling the country, and ultimately found himself here—lost in the middle of a forest, days away from the nearest town, starving and resigned to death. A creature approached him when he collapsed from hunger, and offered him food. In all of his writings, Matthias never revealed the being's name. My family calls it the Shadow Being.

"The food restored Matthias's strength, and having earned the man's trust, the Shadow Being made a proposition. It offered to return Matthias's fortunes fivefold. It said it could provide him with endless wealth, with good fortune, and with unfailing health—not just for Matthias, but for his descendants, too. In return, the creature asked for two things: that Matthias build it a house to its exact specifications and for the use of Matthias's body when he died.

"The proposal seemed to offer so much and request so little in return that Matthias eagerly agreed. The creature made good on its word; it provided Matthias with a fortune—I have no idea how—that allowed him to hire workers to carve a glade in the forest and build Northwood exactly as the Shadow Being requested it. Matthias met and married a woman from town, and they had twelve sons. Each son married and had children of his own, and the Argenton family swelled to fifty members within just two generations.

"The Shadow Being's bargain initially seemed faultless. As promised, the Argenton family prospered financially. Sickness was unheard of while they lived within the house's boundaries, and repeated good fortune came their way. In return, whenever one of the family members passed away, the body would be left for the creature to take."

"If they had good health, how did they pass away?" Sophie asked.

"That's the first of the creature's loopholes. It promised good health, but not safety from calamity. Every one of the Argentons have died a violent death. My great-aunt fell from the balcony. Her husband was murdered by his jealous son. That son was crushed by a felled chandelier. His wife drowned in her bath. Forgive me, Sophie—I didn't mean to distress you."

Sophie had pressed her hand over her mouth, but she took it away with a resolute breath. "I'm fine. Please continue."

Joseph's black eyes scanned hers. "Are you certain?"

"Yes. I want to know the full of it."

"Very well. Although we never see the creature—or, I should say, we see it very infrequently; I've only seen it once in my life— we're frequently aware of its presence. It walks the hallways like us, although it can't be seen. We can hear it breathe when it's nearby."

Sophie thought of the footsteps that had stalked her in those lightless moments in the library, and again in the room that had dripped blood. She suppressed a shiver and nodded for Joseph to continue.

"The second of the bargain's loopholes was what happened to us after death. The Shadow Being claimed it needed to absorb the body's residual energy—what's left after the spirit has gone— as a source of food. As far as I can tell, that's accurate, but it's not the full story. The bodies become reanimated and bent to the creature's will. They are what attacked you in the forest."

She saw Marie lurching out of her wardrobe, sharp teeth exposed, arms stretching toward Sophie's face. *It wore Marie's face, but it was something entirely different.*

Joseph had finished cleaning the blood away from the cuts and applied a salve. "As these detriments became more and more prominent, many of my ancestors became resentful of the bargain. Here is the third and worst loophole: simply by being born into this family, we are considered part of the Shadow Being's bargain. If we try to break the contract—if we leave Northwood—we die."

"But you came to town," Sophie said. "You were there for weeks."

"And that was the limit of what I could endure. Short excursions from Northwood are permissible, as long as you have the intention of returning. But within a few days, you begin to feel unwell. The sickness increases, and if you don't heed it and return to the house, you eventually succumb. I was away for exactly three weeks; that's the longest that has ever been allowed. You remember I had to leave you the same day as our wedding. The sickness had progressed more quickly than I'd expected and forced me to ride almost incessantly to return to Northwood in time."

He looked unwell in the carriage, and the innkeeper had expressed concern over his health, but he seemed fine when he greeted me at Northwood's gates.

"I told you that many of my ancestors died during a splitting of the house. Two paths of thought had developed—those who believed the bargain was still beneficial and those who thought it a toxic, parasitic relationship and wished to be free. This developed into a war. Two factions, trapped in the same house, with building paranoia and mistrust… A great deal of blood was shed over the course of two months. At the end of it, very few of them remained. And that's when the contract began to truly hurt."

Joseph paused for a moment as he bandaged Sophie's arm. During his story, she'd almost forgotten about the cuts. She was surprised to realize she couldn't feel them any longer.

"While the family was large, the Shadow Being took the elderly almost exclusively. There was a death every three or four years, and our numbers were easily replenished with new births. We had balance. But with just a dozen Argentons left and only a couple of them able to bear children, the creature began claiming young lives. It needed to feed just as frequently, but there weren't enough family members left to sustain it. Men and women of all ages—even children—began dying.

"You can imagine the pain this caused to their survivors. While it had been possible to accept the deaths of the elderly as a natural part of life, it was insufferable to lose those who were still young."

Joseph had finished tying the bandage, but his hands lingered on her arm, as though he were reluctant to lose the contact. He still wouldn't meet her eyes. "I was a child during the second massacre. It was begun by the death of my younger sister, who was only a baby. My mother, a good, sweet woman, was crushed with grief. She rallied almost all of her remaining cousins and siblings to join her in a fight against the monster. They intended to kill it and end the contract. But they failed. Weapons pierced its hide but couldn't extinguish its life. And its retaliation was swift and brutal." His eyes fluttered closed. "I was there to see it eat my mother."

The pain in his face was almost too much for Sophie to tolerate. "Joseph…"

He released her arm and sat back on his chair with a bitter smile. "Don't pity me yet, my dear. You haven't heard the full story. Give me a moment."

She didn't like the twisted, pained smile he wore. He poured them both fresh tea and sipped his in silence for a moment. When he spoke again, his voice was thick but steady. "After the failed resistance, there were only four of us left: myself, Aunt Rose, Uncle Garrett, and his wife, Emily."

"Wife? I thought Rose—"

"Rose is Garrett's sister. No, don't be embarrassed—you made a natural assumption about their relationship, and I said nothing to dissuade you from it. It was simpler to not have to explain why both of their partners died young. I shouldn't have concealed it."

"Then Elise…?"

"Garrett's wife, Emily, gave birth to Elise six years after my mother's failed resistance. The Shadow Being hadn't claimed any lives in that time, but it took Emily during childbirth. Following that, we remaining three—Garrett, Rose, and I—came to an accord: we would not inflict our curse on anyone else. The Shadow Being would take us one by one, and when it was done with us, its reign would end.

"I believe the creature has realized our numbers are dangerously reduced, which is why it has allowed us to live undisturbed for the twelve years since Emily's death. It must have hoped one or several of us would marry and produce more heirs. But we haven't, and it began punishing us for our resistance. For these last four months, it has been tormenting Elise."

He stared into his empty teacup as his voice was reduced to a raw whisper. "You've seen the drawings she's produced, and I'm sure you've noticed how unwell she seems. She wakes screaming from bad dreams. She goes into trances. She's stopped eating. We were accepting of her death—of all of our deaths—but it won't come. The message is clear: increase the Argenton family or watch Elise suffer."

He broke off and pressed the back of his hand to his lips. Sophie's heart ached for him; she wanted nothing more than to drop her tea and embrace him, to stroke his brow clear and kiss away his paleness, but she made herself stay still.

"I wasn't strong enough to endure it," he continued. "Watching her suffer day after day while it was within my power to relieve it…so I left for the city with the intention of finding a wife."

Sophie couldn't watch his face anymore. His lips were white, and his black eyes were so full of anger and frustration that it felt like knives slicing through her chest. She focused on her hands instead.

"I never intended to choose a gentleman's daughter. My plan was to find a widow reduced to poverty or a street worker or a lady suffering from an incurable illness—anyone whose life was too miserable for them to have much want of continuing it. But I made a mistake: I took advantage of my brief freedom from Northwood and went to the theater. And I saw *you*."

She dared to look at him and found the gaze returned. Adoration, want, and regret filled his countenance.

185

"You were beautiful. So sweet and gentle. I was captivated. My situation was empty of all of the comfort and joy you seemed to offer. When I looked at you, I imagined what my life could have been like if I weren't tied to Northwood. I would call on you, attend events with you, and attempt to win your affections.

"And in a fit of petulant selfishness, I thought, why *shouldn't* I have some brief happiness in this bleak existence? Why *shouldn't* I enjoy the company of a beautiful woman? And the house knew." He closed his eyes. "The house knew, and it gave you to me."

"The shipping disaster…" Sophie breathed.

"Yes. I didn't ask for it to happen. It was never my wish to harm you or your family. When the event was made known to me the morning I was to visit you, I was furious at myself for my weakness the night before. But it was too late to take back; I could have you as my wife and ensure your family were taken care of or I could leave you fortuneless." He bared his teeth in a humorless smile. "Though I now suspect you might have preferred the latter."

Sophie opened her mouth to reply, but she didn't know what to say. On one side, she would have given almost anything to not have come to Northwood—except cause her family suffering. Her next thought was that she wished she'd never seen Joseph in the first place, but that wasn't honest, either. The fluttering emotion in her chest was beaten and bleeding, but still, it lived.

The fire was growing low, so Joseph rose to throw another log on it. He stood with his back to Sophie as he finished his story. "Most of the rest you already know. The house wouldn't allow me to stay in the city for long, and I dreaded what might happen if I returned to Northwood still unattached, so I married you as quickly as was possible.

"When I set out to find a wife, my plan had been to give her to the Shadow Being the same night we arrived home. Elise's suffering would be alleviated, and we would have peace for at least a few more years. But the more I saw of you, the more impossible that seemed. Do you remember our first dinner together, when I became angry at you for finding the red door? I'm sure you saw me shake my head at Garrett. He had been asking if I was to give you up that night. But I couldn't. And the more I grew to know you, the more agonizing the idea of losing you became."

Sophie wrapped the blanket around herself more tightly. "Elise is still suffering. And she's going to continue to suffer until I die, isn't she?"

Joseph lowered his head. The fire silhouetted his black hair, making it seem even darker than normal. "While I was in the city, I heard something that gave me the smallest seed of hope. A gentleman named Crowther was traveling through the region. He was well known for his research into cryptozoology—that is, the study of creatures that are widely regarded as mythical or fictional. I've been in communication with Mr. Crowther, but he was extremely reluctant to visit Northwood. Even when I offered him most of my fortune, the closest he would come was the nearby town, where he invited me to meet him at the inn."

"That's why you left," Sophie breathed.

"Yes. I had hoped to convince him to return with me to

Northwood. I believed he, above anyone else, might have the knowledge and abilities to defeat or expel the Shadow Being." Joseph finally turned to look at Sophie, but his face was dark. "It was my last hope. If he had been able to help, I could have saved both you and Elise. We could have left Northwood, as you desperately wanted to. I could have put right all that was wrong."

"He didn't come back, though."

Joseph grimaced. "When I arrived at his room, I found him dead. I cannot say what from—whether it was one of the seizures I had heard he suffered from, and unrelated to our situation, or if the house's power had extended to quash him before he could threaten it. I believe it may be the latter, but I hope it was the former. I have enough blood on my hands already."

Sophie's insides felt cold and hollow. She wanted to go to Joseph and feel his arms around her, but she couldn't muster the energy to rise to her feet. "Is it certain I'm tied to the bargain?"

"Yes." He sighed. "By marrying me, you're now a part of the Argenton family. And the Shadow Being has always taken outsiders—that is, those who marry into the family rather than being born into it—first. As I said earlier, I don't expect you to forgive me. But I *will* do everything in my power to protect you."

Sophie let her breath out slowly. All of the questions that had haunted her were either nearly or completely answered, but there was one thing she still wanted to know. "When you left to go hunting, you weren't seeking wolves, were you?"

"No. There are no wolves. I told you that to keep you away from the forest." Joseph turned toward the window, where the treetops were barely visible. "The Shadow Being's pets—the bodies it reanimates—live outside the house. They used to stay in the woods, but since the Shadow Being started punishing Elise, it has allowed the bodies to creep closer to our home. The deer you saw dead below your window was one of their victims. I can't kill the bodies, but if I break them, they take several days to knit back together. I've been hunting them in an attempt to keep them away from you."

"How many are there?"

"More than a hundred Argentons, as well as countless staff members."

Sophie's mind flashed to Marie. "They don't suffer when the creature takes them, do they?"

"I don't believe so. Sophie—" He paused as he struggled to phrase himself. "I'm deeply grieved by what happened to Marie. She was a good woman. I suspect you think I hired her because she was mute. That was a perquisite, but not the deciding factor. She was bright and didn't ask for much to be happy. I'd hoped she would have been a comfort and companion for you. I never wanted her to be hurt any more than I want to see you hurt."

He turned back to the fire. It cast sharp shadows over his face as he folded his arms with a sigh.

CHAPTER 28
FATE

SOPHIE LAPSED INTO SILENCE. There was so much to process that she struggled to untangle her feelings. She knew she should be afraid, distressed, and at least a little angry, but she felt none of those emotions. Instead, there was a profound sense of relief, as though a vice had been loosened from her chest.

Even though the answers were impossibly grim, simply knowing what she faced gave her strength. She wasn't blind anymore. Seeing Northwood for what it really was didn't make it less frightening, but it at least gave her something to fight.

Joseph had said he would understand if she was angry at him, but she wasn't. While he'd been talking, she'd imagined what it would have been like if their roles had been reversed. If Thomas, Lucy, or Bella had been suffering as she'd seen Elise suffer…she didn't like to think about what she would have been prepared to do to save them.

Joseph's explanation was bittersweet. His actions and words finally made sense, and she felt she could stand with him as an equal. More than that, she could *trust* him. But the answers were like surfacing to gasp in a lungful of air in shark-filled waters: the relief only lasted a second before she saw the fins turning toward her.

"It took Marie," she said, thinking the situation through. "Does that mean it no longer needs to eat?"

"I'm afraid not. It will take any body offered to it and will be sated for a day or two, but it still needs a regular death from part of the Argenton family."

"Because of the bargain?"

"I believe so."

Something about Joseph's tone made Sophie lean forward in her seat to get a better look at his expression. He stood close to the fire, and she could see the deep crevices of guilt and fear lining his face.

He thinks I'm angry, she realized with a shock. *He's afraid I'll hate him if he tries to get closer.*

She didn't feel angry, though. The thought of Joseph spending his life inside Northwood's walls made her want to cry for him. When she searched her feelings about the tall, dark man, she felt nothing but a deep, aching love and respect. He was fallible but well-intentioned. He had made terrible choices, but only because someone dear to him had been threatened. Without the house's influence and the constant threat of danger hanging over his head, he would be a truly good man.

"Joseph."

He turned, and she held a hand toward him. He hesitated, and a flash of surprise crossed his face before he moved closer and took her hand. She gently pulled him to sit beside her in the chair and leaned her head against his neck. Slowly and cautiously, Joseph moved his hand around her shoulder to stroke her hair.

What can I say to make him understand? She wanted to say only one thing, though, and she had to collect all of her courage to lean closer and whisper it into his ear. "I love you."

Joseph became still. After a moment, he said, "Are you serious?"

"I—yes." Sophie frowned and pressed her face against his shirt so he couldn't see how red she was. "Why, is that hard to believe?"

"Tonight's conversation has been playing over in my head for the last three days. I had hoped you would accept my company and help. During the morning by the lake, I dreamed you might even forgive me. I had never presumed to hope for love."

There was quiet, stunned wonder in his voice, and Sophie couldn't stop herself from smiling. She tightened her grip on him, and he responded in turn, threading his arms about her and clinging as though his life depended on it.

"I meant it when I said you didn't have to be alone any longer." Sophie's voice was muffled, but she hoped he could still understand her. "We'll fight this together."

He tried to reply then settled on kissing the top of her head. It sent a glowing feeling through her chest, easing away the aches. While she was with him, she felt almost invincible.

"Sophie." He was speaking carefully again, and she inclined

her head to watch his expression. It was anxious and conflicted. "I don't want to mislead you: I have no idea what to do next. I have no plan, no avenues to explore, or advice to seek now that Crowther is gone. Believe me when I say—I will fight for you with every breath I have left. But I'm frightened that won't be enough."

"I know." The glow faded, but in its place developed a grim determination. *There has to be a way out of this. Something we're overlooking…or someone who'll know what to do… I feel like, if I could just piece the puzzle together in the right order, I might be able to help…* "Tell me more about the Shadow Being."

Joseph took a deep breath. "I only saw it once, on the day my mother tried to defeat it. Otherwise, it has very little contact with us. We hear its footsteps on occasion—and sometimes even hear its breathing—but otherwise, it's almost possible to imagine it doesn't live in this house."

"How did your mother fight it?"

"With every weapon we had available. I remember guns, knives, and boiling water. None of them made it so much as flinch."

Sophie chewed her lip. "And the gentleman you tried to visit in town, Crowther: He didn't say anything in his reply letters?"

"Just one thing, which I can't understand. When I found him at the inn, he had my most recent letter open on his desk, with a word written below my farewell. But I don't recognize it."

Joseph shifted to reach into his pocket then offered the letter to Sophie. She scanned Joseph's neatly written message quickly.

He'd laid out the situation in an abridged version of what he'd told Sophie that night and had implored Crowther to meet with him if nothing else. Below Joseph's signature, a very different, far messier hand had scrawled *Grimlock*.

Grimlock… Sophie mouthed. The word was familiar, but she couldn't place it. Then, with a burst of anxious hope, she tugged Marie's drawing from her dress and unfolded it. "This was in my book," she said, breathless.

Joseph leaned closer to see the picture. "That doesn't look like Elise's drawings."

"No, Marie made it not long before Rose took her. She'd opened the red door."

Joseph made a faint noise of shock, and his arm tightened around Sophie. "You said it was in your book?"

"Yes. My father bought me a collection of books when I was a child. One of them was called *Cryptids and the Occult*. I read it all in one sitting, and it gave me nightmares for weeks. One page was titled *Grimlock*, but I can't remember…"

Sophie pressed her palms against her eyes, and Joseph began stroking her hair again. He seemed to understand that she needed silence, and didn't try to interrupt as Sophie scrambled through the half-lost memories.

"The stories were illustrated… That must be why Elise's pictures seemed familiar. Grimlock was the name of the creature. 'It makes bargains with humans…' That's exactly what happened to your family. The book called it 'a deal with the devil.' What were its weaknesses? I can't remember. There was a way to get out of the contract, though... You had to kill it... No, not just kill it... *Destroy its heart.*" Sophie looked up, ecstatic.

Joseph's eyebrows had risen. "Are you certain?"

"N-not completely, but I *think* that's right."

Color and animation flooded Joseph's face. He gripped her shoulders, pulled her close, and kissed her hard. His mouth felt too good; Sophie wrapped her arms about his shoulders and surrendered herself to the sensations. Joseph's hands slipped down to the small of her back and pressed her body against his.

When he pulled back, they were both breathless. Joseph laughed as he peppered kisses across her forehead and cheeks. "How is this possible?" he asked between breaths. "It's like you were sent to save me. Sophie, my darling, I don't think I deserve you."

His laugh was too infectious for Sophie to keep a straight face. His light kisses tickled and sent a hot sensation flowing through her, and she couldn't stop laughing until Joseph finally relented.

"I just wish I could remember more from the book," she said.

"Even so—this is more than I've been able to find out from any other source. I ordered in hundreds of books and wrote to anyone I thought could help. The priest was convinced it was a demon, and wouldn't step inside the house. But this—ha, my dear, I think we might actually stand a chance."

His voice had grown hard again, and although his fingers continued to caress her lower back, his eyes were flickering over the dancing fire as he thought. Sophie kept still. There was something deeply intense—even hungry—about Joseph's face.

Her news had washed away the defeat and anxiety, and in its place, the wolf had woken.

Sophie had heard other women say they found power attractive, but the power they talked about always involved external gifts—dukes and lords born into a privileged position. Sophie had never understood how such a shallow advantage could be attractive.

But this was *true* power. Joseph was strong, intelligent, and desperate enough to fight his quarter despite the odds. This was the power that turned gladiators into victors in the Colosseum, and kept the wolf from starving during a long winter. And Sophie had never seen anything so electrically, beautifully engrossing.

The distance in Joseph's eyes faded, and he turned back to Sophie just in time to catch her expression. He smiled then pulled her close to kiss her again. He was more tender than before, and he brushed his thumb over her cheek as he pulled back. "Can you bear to stay in this house for another few days?"

"I—" Sophie, still focused on the kiss, had to shake her mind back to their present situation. She looked at the window. The moon had risen above the roof, but she was still very aware that they were surrounded by woods filled with the living dead. As long as Joseph held her, she felt safe from the house and everything it contained. But they couldn't spend every minute together, and those brief separations terrified her. "I don't know."

Joseph's black eyes transfixed her. "I understand. But the house will be sated for at least a little while after today's sacrifice, and I feel it would be wise to plan our attack carefully."

"Yes, of course." Sophie felt faintly embarrassed that she'd been imagining an offensive that very night. Joseph's closeness had made her feel invincible. But she knew he was right—they needed to plan and prepare.

The keen, thoughtful look had returned to Joseph's eyes. "I'm fairly certain I can convince Garrett to join us."

Sophie remembered how Garrett had callously discussed Marie's death in front of her after leaving Marie at the red door, and she suppressed a shudder. She wasn't sure she wanted him as an ally. "Not Rose, though?"

"No. We will need to keep this a secret from Rose." Joseph sighed and resumed stroking Sophie's hair. She had the feeling the motion was as much a comfort for him as it was for her. "When my mother tried to attack the Shadow Being—the Grimlock, I should say—she was able to convince almost all of the family to join her. Those who stayed behind had different reasons; Garrett was recently married, and his wife, who feared the Grimlock, begged Garrett not to leave her. I wanted to join the fight, but my mother thought I was too young, and she left me in Garrett's charge. Rose had a very different motive, though—she was the last of the Argentons who believed the Grimlock's bargain was a gift to be cherished. She wanted us to continue as we always had, to rebuild our numbers and revel in our position as one of the wealthiest families in the country."

Sophie frowned. "I can't believe she'd side with a monster."

"Rose wanted to believe our family was gifted, rather than cursed. She agreed that the price was steep, but unlike the rest of us, she thought that it was a fair exchange for the privilege we experienced. However, she was very close to my mother, her sister, and grieved heavily after her death. For some time now, I've suspected she has had the beginnings of mental instability. Only recently has that become clear." Joseph kissed Sophie's forehead again. "I'm deeply sorry I had to leave you with her."

"But you think Garrett will stand with us?"

"He knows he has very little to lose. Even if the Grimlock took one of our family, it would only be a temporary solution. The Grimlock would be quiet for three or possibly four years, but then the tormenting would begin again. Even if we expanded the Argenton family as the beast hopes, the trials of watching loved ones perish would eventually fall to Elise. Garrett might save her for a few years, but ultimately, Elise's life would be as painful and bleak as his own has been."

And yours, too. Sophie tightened her grip on his shirt.

"I doubt he will hope for much success, but Garrett will almost certainly fight alongside us. He has a good heart and cares for his family above all else."

"There will be three of us, then," Sophie said. "We should make a plan. Would you like to wake Garrett and ask him tonight, or would it be better to wait until tomorrow?" She didn't like the expression on Joseph's face. She'd seen it before; he was trying to find the words to introduce a subject he knew she wouldn't like. "What's wrong?"

Joseph chuckled and gave her a smile. "Truthfully, I'd prefer it if there were just *two* of us."

"Oh. But you said Garrett—"

"I mean I would be happier knowing *you* were somewhere safe. Away from the fight."

I should have expected this. Sophie frowned at the arm encircling her. She could feel Joseph's muscles through the shirt. He was lean but strong, and he could fight. She'd seen that herself in the forest. Conversely, Sophie had never lifted a hand in aggression. Every ounce of logic in her body agreed that she would be more of a risk than a help if she joined the fight.

Still, she couldn't agree with her husband's request. As soon as her mind traveled near the idea of losing Joseph, blind panic filled her. *I can't lose him. Not now that I love him so dearly.* She'd increased her grip on Joseph's arm without realizing, and his free hand moved to stroke her fingers until she loosened her hold.

"I want to be with you," Sophie said. Her voice was hoarse, and she licked her lips before continuing. "Whatever the outcome."

Joseph took her hand from his arm and kissed the backs of her fingers one at a time. "I don't want us to disagree," he murmured. "Especially not tonight. Let's revisit this tomorrow."

Sophie relaxed and nodded. "Tomorrow."

"We can talk to Garrett then, too. We'll work better with clear minds."

He'd pressed her hand to his chest, and Sophie could feel his heartbeat. It was a good, strong tempo. She smiled and nodded. "Is it very late?"

"After midnight. I would stay up until morning talking with you, but I'm afraid we need sleep."

"That's sensible." Sophie's smile faltered. She thought of her own room, cold and dark, with the damned wardrobe in the corner. *What if Marie returns?*

Joseph saw her expression, and he strengthened his grip on her hand. "Would you like to stay with me tonight?"

"Yes!" Sophie turned red as she realized, too late, how eager she'd sounded.

Joseph chuckled. "You can have the bed. I'll sleep in the chair." When Sophie didn't answer, Joseph nudged her chin up so that he could see her expression, and a curious smile grew over his lips. He bent toward her, very slowly and carefully, to kiss where her neck curved into her shoulder. "*Or* we could figure out another arrangement…"

"Yes," Sophie breathed, arching into his touch. She was rewarded with the sensation of Joseph's hands wrapping about her back and pressing her closer to him as he kissed her hungrily.

CHAPTER 29
NIGHT

JOSEPH'S FINGERS TRACED PATTERNS across Sophie's back as they lay, limbs tangled, in his bed. He was breathing heavily, and his skin was still damp with sweat. He felt solid and strong, and the way he'd wrapped his arms about her made Sophie feel completely enveloped.

Sophie let her own hands explore his chest in quiet wonder. Joseph was smiling at her. He was tired, but there was so much adoration in his expression that she almost couldn't stand it. He shifted closer to kiss the top of her head and mumbled, almost too quietly for her to hear, "Love you."

The words sent a shiver of heat through Sophie, and she smiled to herself as she pressed her fingers over his broad shoulders. The cuts from the previous day still marred his chest, but what had been scabbed wounds the previous morning had healed into faint red scores. They were almost invisible, and it took her a moment to remember the reason for his quick recovery. "Your cuts are much better," she said, drawing a finger over the red mark. "Is that because of the bargain?"

"Yes." He was almost asleep but continued to trace patterns over her naked back. "One of the few perquisites. Your own cuts should be much better by tomorrow, too."

Tomorrow. The thought risked cutting through her happy glow. *Tomorrow we'll have to face the Grimlock. Do we really have any hope?*

"My dear," Joseph said, bringing his hand up to caress her jaw. "Are you frightened?"

She opened her mouth to say no, but didn't speak. Their game of secrets and lies had ended, and she didn't want the start of their new closeness to be filled with any untruths. "Yes. I don't want you to be hurt."

He pulled her closer and wrapped the blankets around her a little more tightly. Sophie found it impossible to stay tense when he was so close, and she relaxed against him.

"I understand," he said. "Put it out of your mind, if you can. We'll face it in the morning." He gave her another gentle kiss. "You're the best thing that's ever happened to me, my darling. I'll do whatever it takes to keep you safe."

His tone unsettled Sophie. Something in the words didn't bode well. She was too tired to chase it, though. *I'll ask him tomorrow. Joseph's right; tonight has been too good to ruin with worry. I should enjoy what I have now.*

Sophie kissed Joseph's warm chest and felt him murmur

happily. At that moment, everything felt right. She felt loved, warm, and secure, and she soaked up the feelings. Joseph's caresses continued until he fell asleep a few minutes later. Sophie listened to his smooth, even breathing and pressed her hand over his heart. Its beat was strong, and she closed her eyes, rejoicing in the sensation as she let her own tiredness pull her into a deep sleep.

CHAPTER 30
THE LETTER

SHE'D BEEN DREADING MORNING'S arrival, but it was still night when Sophie woke. Pale-blue moonlight sifted through the window, bathing the room in its cold glow. Joseph no longer lay next to her.

Sophie startled upright. Even though the fire was still crackling, the air felt cold on her skin, and she pulled the blankets around her torso as she scanned the room for her husband. She was alone.

"No…"

Panic shoved away any remnants of tiredness. Sophie stumbled out of bed and scrambled to retrieve her dress from where Joseph had discarded it on the floor. It was dirty and scuffed from her experience in the forest, and Sophie felt heat flush her cheeks as she realized she must have looked terrible the night before.

Joseph hadn't noticed, though. She remembered the way he'd looked at her—as though she were the most captivating woman in the country—and her heart skipped a beat.

Where is he? Why did he leave?

She turned on the spot as she struggled into the dress. The clock on the mantel read a little after three in the morning. The fire was bright and hot, which meant Joseph must have put new wood on it while she was sleeping.

Then Sophie caught sight of a piece of paper folded neatly on Joseph's pillow. She ran to pick it up then carried it back to the fire to read it in the warm glow.

My Dearest Sophie,

I wish I could say this to you in person, but I know you wouldn't have let me leave. I have already asked for an unreasonable amount of forgiveness today, and I'm afraid I must now ask for more.

You said I didn't have to be alone. Those words have meant more to me than you can imagine, and they have given me strength and focus. But I cannot, in good conscience, allow you to fight my battles.

You were brought into this house through my own selfish choices. I caused you suffering and condemned you to a fate no person deserves. I cannot ask you for any other sacrifice. The remedy should be mine and mine alone.

I have gone to fight the Grimlock. If you're reading this note, it means I have failed. Leave Northwood immediately. I believe that my death will bring about the end of your part in the Argenton contract.

There are two ways to enter the bargain: by birth and by marriage. The Grimlock has always taken those who married into the family before taking their partners, and I have begun to suspect this means that the end of your marriage—by my death—will free you from the curse.

There is a pouch of money on the writing table. Take it, and have Garrett arrange the carriage for you. It will take you as far as the local town, where you can hire a coach and travel to your father's. You should be safe once you are outside Northwood's gates.

I am leaving you tonight with the intention of succeeding and giving us a future together. But I am also fully prepared for the worst. I didn't want to say anything last night, while you were so hopeful, but I fear destroying the Grimlock's heart may not be as easy as it sounds. When my mother led the attack against it, they used swords and bullets to pierce its hide. The Grimlock showed no signs of pain or fear over the assault. That makes me suspect the book was misled as to the method for killing the Grimlock. Still—I must try.

My dearest Sophie, words cannot express how much I feel for you. During our time together, you have made me happier than I ever thought possible. My only regret is not being able to be with you longer. Do not grieve for me any more than you need to. All that I ask is for you to be safe and as happy as is possible.

My deepest regard and love,
Joseph

Sophie dropped the letter and pressed both hands over her face. She couldn't breathe. Terror and overwhelming horror threatened to drown her.

He can't be gone.

She stood and crossed the room. A pouch sat on the writing table, as Joseph had said it would. It looked full and heavy; he'd given her a small fortune.

He can't leave me.

The letter lay where she'd dropped it in front of the fire. The flames reflected off the ink, making the shimmering words seem almost alive. Sophie was faintly aware of how carefully the message must have been written. Joseph had kept his promise of honesty, but he'd given Sophie no chance to change his mind.

She'd always sensed the Argentons could be capable of terrible things, and her premonition had been proven right. Rose murdered glibly. Garrett could observe death without emotion. And Joseph could disregard his own life and shred her heart, if he thought it would save her.

No, no, no, please, no—

How long ago had he left? Was there a chance he might still return? It was night, and the fire had been fed no more than an hour before. And yet, Sophie knew it was a faint hope. Whatever battle ensued from the confrontation must be resolved quickly; if Joseph had been able to return to her, he already would have.

Tears coursed down her cheeks, but Sophie did nothing to stop them. Nearly a day before, she would have given anything to be free from Northwood. But now that she'd been given a clear escape, walking alone through the front door felt worse than any mortal death.

I have to find him.

Sophie pushed through the doors. The lamps lining the hallway had long since been extinguished, and she could only see a few feet ahead of herself in the fire's light. Beyond that, the darkness seemed to stretch for miles, and the house felt more alive than it ever had before.

Not because it's been fed. Don't even think that.

Sophie ran back to the room and pulled her boots on as quickly as she could, then she snatched the candle from the writing desk and lit it in the fire. She cast about for a weapon and settled on a letter opener resting among Joseph's stationery. She knew a proper knife or even a gun from downstairs would have been a better choice, but she didn't have time to retrieve one. Every wasted moment pulled Joseph farther away from her. She had to find him—no matter the consequences—and she already knew where to look.

She ran through the hallways with one hand held in front of the candle's flame to shield it from the stirring air. She knew Joseph had gone to the red door. *The burial ground for countless bodies. The source of Joseph's fear for me during our first dinner together. The door that seems to quietly whisper.*

The tall, red wooden divider filled her with dread, but worse than that was the terror of what could have happened to Joseph on its other side.

I can't lose him now.

The red door had always seemed to appear when she was least expecting it, but now that she was actually searching for the black hallway, it seemed impossible to find. Sophie ran until she was breathless and a stitch developed in her side. She thought she might be going in circles, but it would have been hard to tell during the day, let alone in the dark.

She leaned against the wall to drag air into her raw lungs. The house was deathly quiet, and everywhere she looked seemed to be a mess of writhing shadows.

Then the music started. It was just one note at first, held for a long time and quickly followed by another and another, until the notes cascaded together into the dreadful, jarring tune.

Sophie pushed away from the wall. The song seemed to come from all directions at once. She closed her eyes and slowly rotated until the sound's location solidified, then she stretched a hand toward it and began walking, trusting her ears to lead her.

The music grew louder as Sophie drew closer. She could sense the song was nearing its end, and she broke into a run. It led her to an unfamiliar door. She sucked in a deep breath and pressed into the room as the tune built into a terrible crescendo. The room was large and empty, save for a single piano sitting in its center. At the piano, eyes half-closed and face slack, sat Rose, looking as though she were in a trance. She didn't look toward the open door or seem aware of her surroundings. Her heavy-lidded eyes were unfocussed, and she swayed slightly as her fingers pounded out the music.

Sophie's heart felt ready to explode. She crept closer until she stood nearly opposite Rose, but the older woman showed no signs of recognition. Despite the late hour, she wore one of her decadent gowns and had strings of pearls slung around her neck. Pure, hot fury rose in Sophie's chest, and she slammed her open palm onto the piano's keys. A deafening *clang* filled the room, interrupting the song, and Rose drew her hands away from the keys with a start.

Her eyes finally met Sophie's, and Rose blinked. The cool control crept back into her face, and the deadness returned to her eyes. "Well, hello, my dear. Couldn't you sleep?"

If she was surprised to see Sophie had returned from the forest, she didn't show it. Sophie suspected Rose had already been aware of Joseph's rescue, in the same way that she seemed aware of everything that happened in the house.

"Show me to the red door," Sophie said, and a viciously delighted smile spread Rose's red-stained lips.

CHAPTER 31
THROUGH THE DOOR

ROSE'S SHOES CLICKED ON the floor as she led Sophie at a brisk pace. Sophie could feel her aunt's frequent glances, but she refused to return them. Asking Rose's assistance scorched her, but it was the fastest way to find Joseph—and she couldn't waste any more time.

"My nephew spoke with you, I suppose?" Rose asked, her voice smoother than honey. Sophie could have almost smiled if she hadn't been so familiar with the stings.

"Yes." She kept her eyes focused ahead. *We can't be far away, can we?*

"Hmm." Rose gave her another sideways glance, this time scanning her from head to foot.

Sophie realized too late that her hands were shaking, and she clenched them to keep them still.

A strange smile curled Rose's lips. "It seems I underestimated you, my dear."

What does she mean?

Rose held her lamp above her head to illuminate more of the passageways. "It shows great moral strength to accept your destiny so readily."

Wait... She doesn't know Joseph has already gone to the door, does she? Rose must think I'm giving myself to the Grimlock as a willing sacrifice.

"And it was wise to go at night, when Joseph can't..." Rose hesitated. "Well, when he can't second-guess his duty to his family."

Should I tell her? No, Joseph said it should be a secret.

"It was the right choice," Rose said, with a hint of maternal pride in her voice. It made Sophie's skin crawl. "Trust me, you wouldn't have lasted long if you'd fought the house. This way will be quick. It's better for everyone."

She'd stopped walking, and Sophie found herself facing the black hallway. The deep-red color at its end was barely visible in the flickering flames.

Fear clenched Sophie's insides into a tight ball. She took a half step down the hallway, but couldn't go farther. She turned back to see Rose's bared teeth glittering in the light, and couldn't stop herself from asking, "What's through the door?"

"Why don't you find that out for yourself?" Rose purred.

Sophie turned back to the hallway and squeezed her eyes closed. Joseph's face rose in her mind's eye, and in a second, her whole world was reduced to his warm smile, his sharp jaw and high cheekbones, and the sparkling delight in his eyes.

Don't hesitate. He needs you.

Sophie started walking, hesitantly at first, then picking up speed as she neared the door. She heard the whispers buzzing just beyond her ability to make out the words. The black handle seemed to sparkle, and she focused on it as she stretched out her hand. The metal was cold under her fingers, but she didn't allow herself the luxury of hesitation. She turned the stiff handle, took a quick breath, and stepped through the door.

CHAPTER 32
ECHOES

SOPHIE'S IMMEDIATE IMPRESSION WAS that she'd somehow become turned around and was facing the wrong direction. A long hallway with dark wallpaper, almost identical to the one she'd just come down, stretched ahead of her. However, Rose no longer stood at its end.

She turned to see behind herself and had a half-second glimpse of Rose's wild smile glittering in the dim light before the door slammed. Sophie jolted away from it, tightened her grip on the candle's holder, and turned back to her path.

Caution told her to move slowly, but fear for Joseph made her take long, quick strides to the hallway's end. It opened onto a new passageway, this one with red-and-gold wallpaper, just like the rest of the house.

No...there's something off about it...

The wallpaper was mirrored, Sophie realized. In the main

house, the paper was red with a gold pattern. These walls were gold with red decorations. The effect was both disorienting and strangely disturbing.

Sophie turned left. Doors and more hallways branched off to either side. She chose turns at random, praying they would lead her to Joseph. Then she caught sight of movement ahead and slowed. What seemed to be a person was crouched on the wooden floor, and it was rocking, not unlike how she'd seen Rose rock while playing the piano. Sophie crept closer and raised her candle to see it clearly. A floorboard creaked under her feet, and the being swiveled to hiss at her.

Thin, pocked skin stretched tightly over the corpse's skull. Its empty eye sockets fixed on Sophie for a second, then it sprang out of its crouch and began to scuttle toward her with deceptive speed.

Sophie gasped and staggered backward. The corpse was too fast to outrun. She remembered how Joseph had beaten them into fragments the day before, and she raised her foot with a terrified wince. The creature reared up to snatch at her, and Sophie brought her boot down on its skull with all of the strength she could muster. Her heel broke through the bone and imploded the beast's head. A plume of black, dust-filled air spewed from the gaping hole, and Sophie stumbled away from the creature.

Its head had been crushed, but the body wasn't dead. It thrashed, flipping from side to side as its bony fingers clawed at where its face had once been, then it stretched its arms toward Sophie once more.

She turned and ran. The awful sound of bony limbs scraping over the wooden floor followed her. Sophie didn't dare look back, hoping the injury had disoriented the cadaver enough that it wouldn't be able to catch her.

More shapes loomed out of the shadows ahead. Pulling up before she collided with them, she reeled backward. Her flame flickered and threatened to go out as half a dozen paste-white faces turned toward their prey.

Sophie backed away from the creatures. The scuttling behind her had become louder, and she glanced over her shoulder to see the half-headed corpse was nearly on top of her. Between her and it, though, was a door. Sophie ran for it as hands snatched at her neck and caught in her hair. She shrieked and threw herself forward to pull free. The door burst open as she slammed into it, and Sophie fell to the ground. The impact winded her, and her candle gave out for a second, smothering her in darkness, before it regained the spluttering, weakened flame. Sophie flipped over to see the white faces trying to follow her through the doorway, and she impulsively kicked at the door. It slammed into the bodies, forcing them back, and she kicked again to close it. A hand had reached through the opening, and it severed from its body with a jarring crunch. Black smoke billowed from the twitching limb as it tumbled to the ground and made grabbing motions in Sophie's direction.

Sophie pulled her legs under herself to keep them clear from the hand. It refused to die, despite being parted from its body. The fingers repeatedly twitched in her direction as it tried to jerk itself closer.

She picked up the candle, feeling immensely grateful that it hadn't died. There weren't any other lights in that part of the house, and the idea of being trapped in the dark made her sick.

What's keeping the hand alive? The creatures in the forest died when they were broken. Sophie, against her better judgment, crawled closer. Strange, sooty smoke drifted away from the severed wrist in thick tendrils. Sophie inclined the candle closer to see it more clearly then gasped as the hand made an abrupt thrashing motion. The index finger grazed her flame, and the fire caught and spread until it engulfed the appendage. The smoke, which had been wispy and dusty before, became thick and black as it spewed from the burning fingers. Sophie stared at it, too horrified to move, until the flames faded, leaving nothing but soot where the hand had once been.

She could hear faint noises through the door. Scratching, scraping sounds, like fingernails on wood, were accompanied by raspy breaths. She stumbled to her feet, willing her legs to hold her weight, and turned to see the room.

It was bleeding. Dark-red liquid dribbled down the walls in thick streaks and pooled on the floor. Sophie's mind seized up as memories of her previous experience threatened to overwhelm her. She closed her eyes, blocking out the sight, and recalled Joseph's face as he'd carried her away from the blood-soaked room, his eyes hard and full of anxiety. The way he'd cradled her against his body, even though she'd been drenched in gore. His soft, calming voice, murmuring words she hadn't heard.

He would save me from this if he could. But right now, I need to be strong for him.

Sophie opened her eyes. There was a door at the opposite side of the room, though it was surrounded by a curtain of blood. She held the candle high, straightened her back, and willed her legs to move her forward. The handle was coated with blood. Sophie tried not to look at it as she fixed her hand around the cold, wet surface and turned it. Her stomach threatened to revolt, but the door opened without resistance. Sophie stepped through quickly and found herself in another hallway.

This looks familiar.

She turned left and thought she recognized the door at the end. She went to it as she wiped her bloodied hand clean on the already-stained dress. She then sucked in a deep breath and opened the door.

A huge window filled the wall opposite. *The favored view. This is my room. And yet…it's not.*

The furniture was gone, save for the wardrobe in the corner. There was something wrong with the cupboard, though; it was the same size and color as Sophie's, but the wood was decayed and crumbling, and black stains spread out behind it to grow across the walls like weeds.

Sophie moved toward the window. The woods were visible in a strange, sickly green light. The trees were all dead and empty. Black branches stretched high above Northwood's roof, creating jagged matrixes across the tinted sky.

It's like a mirror dimension. The same house, but changed.

A creak startled Sophie, and she turned. The wardrobe door was inching open. A slender, white hand stretched through the gap, and Sophie stumbled away from it.

"No, please…"

Marie's dead face followed the hand as she crawled out of her home. She was fresher than the other corpses and still recognizable. But there was nothing friendly about the gaze she turned on Sophie. Her mouth opened to expose the rows of pointy teeth as she took a rocking, erratic step forward.

What has this house done to you?

A faint hiss escaped the open mouth. Sophie skittered backward into the hallway and slammed the door behind herself.

"I'm so sorry, Marie," she whispered. A scrabbling, scratching noise came through the wood as the corpse tried to claw its way out of the room.

Sophie stepped away from the closed door. Her heart ached, and her limbs were weak and shaking. She wiped sweat away from her face then turned back to the hallway. *If this is a mirror of Northwood, I should be able to explore through it. Where should I look, though? Where would Joseph go?*

She didn't dare call for him. The corpses seemed to respond to noise, and she couldn't risk attracting more.

Would he stay on the third floor? Or maybe go to the dining room, or the kitchens…?

Sophie clasped the candle in front of herself. She only knew one path through Northwood—the way from her room to the staircase—so that was the path she took.

She moved quickly but cautiously and glanced around corners before passing them. She thought she could hear the corpses' faint scratching noises deep in the building, but otherwise, Northwood was quiet.

She'd never hated the mansion as much as she did at that moment. The mirrored red-and-gold wallpaper was sickening. The air left a bad taste on her tongue. Every creak and distant groan made her shiver. But she couldn't leave until she'd found Joseph—even if she had to search the entire building.

A strange blue light came from farther ahead, where the passageway opened onto the stairs. Sophie slowed to a creep as she edged nearer, then she bent forward to look around the wall's corner.

The foyer, normally a cold, empty expanse, had been decorated with rows of torches around its perimeter. Their flames had an alien blue-white tint, which only barely lit the room. The tiles had changed to a deep-black shade, which gave Sophie the impression of a dark, shiny lake. A rifle lay discarded not far from the base of the stairs. In the center of the foyer crouched the Grimlock, with Joseph crumpled at its feet.

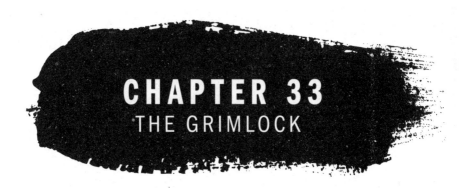

CHAPTER 33
THE GRIMLOCK

SOPHIE CLAMPED HER HAND over her mouth to smother her cry. Joseph lay on his back, his arms spread and eyes closed. He wasn't moving.

The Grimlock bent low over Joseph's torso, its jaws working as it ate him. It pulled away with a sickeningly wet tearing noise and raised its head to stare at Sophie.

It was a thousand times worse than the drawings had prepared her for. Naked, all glistening black and nearly twice as tall as a man, the Grimlock could have stepped out of her worst night-mares. Instead of fingers, long, sharp claws extended from its hands. It crouched and moved like an animal, but the two large, glowing white eyes held a cruel human intellect. Sharklike teeth, which dripped blood, filled its maw.

Joseph's blood.

Sophie screamed. She stumbled down the stairs recklessly, but her legs failed her on the last step, and she collapsed to the floor. A high-pitched ringing noise filled her ears, and her limbs felt numb.

He can't be dead. He can't.

The Grimlock rose from its prey, and an icy chuckle filled Sophie's ears as it stepped over Joseph. "Good morning, little lamb." Its voice sounded like bone being dragged across stone; it was deep and cruel and made Sophie flinch. "Such a pleasure to finally meet you in person."

Unable to bring herself to look at the Grimlock, she focused on Joseph. His face was dead-white. She couldn't tell if he was still breathing.

The Grimlock took a languid pace closer. It moved with animalistic grace, but bent low so that it could scrape its claws across the black marble. "You've made such a poor choice tonight, my pretty," it murmured, grinning. "Your dear husband bought your freedom with his life. There was nothing I could have done to prevent you from leaving my home if you'd tried. But now, look—you've negated his sacrifice by *giving* yourself to me. So thoughtful. I've starved these last eighteen years; tonight I will feast."

Hot, raging fury filled Sophie. Between the pain, her terror for Joseph, and her hatred for the creature in front of her, no room for fear remained. She pulled the letter opener free from where she'd hidden it in her dress and ran at the Grimlock.

Its maw widened into a vicious smile, and it spread its arms, as though welcoming her attack. Sophie hit its chest with all the strength she possessed and plunged the blade deep into where the heart should have been.

She felt the Grimlock's cold, slimy flesh under her fingers. Its breath, saturated with rot, washed over her. Sophie released the blade and staggered backward.

The Grimlock raised its claws, fixed them around the letter opener, and drew the blade from its breast. The knife clattered to the floor. A hole fluttered open in the beast's chest, then the skin began to knit back together, closing the wound as the Grimlock's laughter filled the foyer.

"Well, well, you have some fight in you after all," it purred, then swiped Sophie aside with a flick of its hand.

The impact tossed Sophie through the air. She slammed into the floor and skidded over the tiles before coming to rest against one of the pillars. A burning pain flashed across her ribs, and she coiled over as she fought to drag air into her lungs. Her eyes watered, blinding her.

The Grimlock stretched, arching its back, then began stalking closer. "It's been a pleasure, dear Sophie," it cooed. "You'll forgive me if I finish this before we can know each other more. Your novelty is wearing off, and I would greatly like to make use of your primary purpose—*food.*"

Its claws fixed around her torso and lifted her until her feet dangled above the ground. Sophie tried to beat the hand away, but the pain was debilitating, and the Grimlock was too thick-skinned to feel her punches.

It opened its red-streaked mouth, then a crack split the air, and

Sophie dropped to the ground. Her leg twisted under her, and her stomach heaved, but she managed to roll backward to get clear of the Grimlock. Looking up, she saw a hole had appeared in the center of its head. The lamp-white eyes widened in surprise as it turned. Sophie followed its gaze, and what she saw could have made her cry.

Joseph had dragged himself across the tile, leaving a streak of blood in his wake, to reach the gun. He couldn't stand—or even sit—but he'd rolled onto his side and propped the gun over his arm to aim at the Grimlock.

The intense, wolflike desperation filled his eyes as they met Sophie's. He opened his mouth, and dark blood flooded from it as he rasped a single word: "*Run.*"

He re-aimed the gun and fired a second time. A fresh hole appeared in the Grimlock's neck, burrowing directly through its spine. The creature didn't even flinch.

"You're tenacious, aren't you, Joseph?" The holes were already knitting together as the Grimlock abandoned Sophie. "You must be *very* fond of her."

Joseph fired a third time. Sophie saw the hole appear in the Grimlock's back and heard the clicking noise as the bullet lodged in one of the marble pillars behind her. The Grimlock bent, plucked the gun from Joseph's hands, broke it in half, and discarded the scraps.

This is all my fault, Sophie thought as she watched the final hole repair itself. Sickening despair rose in her stomach. *I thought its heart was its weakness—but it's not. It can't be killed. And now Joseph is going to die because of my advice.*

The Grimlock brought its foot down on Joseph, slamming him into the ground. Joseph gasped in pain, but it was a weak, barely there noise. The Grimlock crouched low over him to whisper, "I'm in no hurry. You know, she doesn't need to be alive for me to consume her. I've always liked you, Joseph; I think I'll let you watch her die."

Joseph's eyes widened in abject terror. Sophie tried to stand, but the burning pain in her chest kept her from straightening, and dizziness made her topple back to the floor.

"Come, my pretties," the Grimlock cooed to the darkness, and the scuttling, scraping noises of a hundred desiccated corpses suddenly filled the room. "Have some fun."

The ghostly shapes materialized at the edges of the blue flames' light. Countless empty eyes fixed on Sophie as the dead began hissing their delight. The closer ones crouched and began creeping toward her.

Joseph was fighting, but the Grimlock was too strong.

"How long do you think she'll scream?" the Grimlock whispered.

No, we can't die. Not like this.

Sophie looked to one side. There was one small splash of color in the otherwise cold blue room: the candle she'd dropped at the foot of the stairs still flickered, its pale-golden flame glowing like a beacon.

The corpses burn, she remembered, and lunged toward the light.

Dead skin grazed her arms as the creatures snatched at her.

Sophie threw herself forward with everything she had. Hands fixed around her ankles, tumbling her to the ground. She glanced behind herself, but there were too many of the dead for her to fight her way free; instead, she rolled onto her stomach. The candle sat barely two feet ahead. She dragged herself closer, using her sweat-dampened palms to pull herself over the floor. The bodies crawled up her legs and scrabbled at her back, their weight forcing the air from her lungs.

"Do you really think you can escape?" The Grimlock's scraping voice rose into smug laughter.

It thinks I'm trying to get to the stairs. Sophie threw her arm forward and felt the warm wax cylinder under her fingers. *Let's see what it thinks of this.*

She stabbed the candle at the closest corpse. The body was so dry that it responded like fine kindling; the flame caught, plumed, and spread across the torso. The corpse wailed and threw itself away from the candle, bumping into its companions and unintentionally spreading the flame.

Sophie rolled onto her back and waved her flame across the corpses clinging to her legs. Shrieking filled the foyer, echoing off the walls and high ceiling and making Sophie squint against the noise.

The Grimlock's bellow cut through the wails. "What have you done?" Abandoning all elegance, it bounded toward her, its face contorted in rage…and *fear*. Its glowing eyes widened as its maw stretched. "*Stupid child, I'll see you suffer for this.*"

The burning corpses were spreading; they had crowded

so tightly around Sophie that the fire leaped across them like lightning. They fled for the shadows as they shrieked, blindly bumping into each other and trailing huge clouds of inky black smoke and hot embers.

The Grimlock screamed and bounded after the bodies. It seemed to be trying to corral them back into the foyer. Some part deep in Sophie's mind thought this had to be significant, but her fear for Joseph pushed aside every conscious idea. She crawled to him and pressed a hand to his cheek.

His eyes fluttered. His breathing was a sick, rattling noise. Sophie glanced about the room and felt tears rise as she saw how much blood he'd spilled. She brushed his sweat-slicked hair away from his forehead and gave him a shaky smile. "Hold still. You're going to be all right."

His hand found hers and pressed it as he wheezed, "Get out."

"Not without you."

Sophie stroked his face as she looked around the foyer. The fiery corpses had spread through the house, but she knew they wouldn't stay lit for long—the hand had burned away within a minute. How long would a full body take?

She guessed they likely had only seconds before the Grimlock returned, and both she and Joseph had to find somewhere safe before then. But Joseph couldn't stand, and she wasn't strong enough to carry him. *Can I make a pallet and pull him on it? But the red door is on the third floor—I can't get him up the stairs like that.*

"Get out," Joseph begged. He took her hand from his face and tried to push her away, but Sophie didn't move.

"We'll be fine. I just need a minute!"

Panic choked her mind. She couldn't see any way to move Joseph—let alone move him *safely*. His shirt was shredded, and she couldn't bring herself to see how bad the injuries underneath were. For all she knew, he might already be as good as dead.

Don't think that. You've come this far—he can't leave you now.

Smoke was filling the room, making it hard to see and stinging Sophie's nose. She could still hear the corpses burning in the distance.

Wait...not the corpses. Something larger.

Sophie looked over her shoulder, toward the dining room. A deep-golden glow flickered through the doorway.

The house has caught on fire. I should have expected it to—there's so much old wood in this building, and the corpses were bumping into furniture and the walls.

Then a new sound drowned out every other noise. It was a deep, protracted, bestial wail, filled with fury, terror, and pain.

The Grimlock.

That was when the clues fell into place for Sophie. *The book said to destroy the Grimlock's heart. But what if the heart isn't a literal physical organ? What if it was meant to be symbolic, such as a vital and cherished object? A house, for instance. A house that was built to the Grimlock's minutely detailed specifications. A house that sometimes feels* alive. *A house that* bleeds.

"Northwood is its heart," Sophie breathed.

The flames were spreading. She could hear the fire's roar coming from multiple doorways and mingling with the Grimlock's screams. Joseph's eyes had closed. His breath had become shallow gasps. Sophie pressed a kiss on his forehead, and a smile twitched at the corners of his mouth.

Maybe it wouldn't be bad to die like this. The Grimlock didn't win. The house didn't claim us. We fought back, and our deaths bring about our victory.

She could run, as Joseph wanted her to, and she thought she could reach the third floor and find the red door before the fire overtook her. But that would mean a future without Joseph. The small emotion that had once fluttered weakly in her chest had attached itself to her heart then spread through her veins to every part of her body like a beautiful, perfect poison.

I wouldn't be sad to die with him.

Sophie leaned onto her side so that she lay next to Joseph. She put her head into the crook of his neck, placed her hand on his shoulder, and closed her eyes. As long as the Grimlock didn't return first—and she thought it would be too preoccupied trying to save the house—the smoke would simply pull them into a sleep they would never wake from.

With her eyes closed, she was able to focus on the small sounds and sensations. Joseph's heart still beat. The pulse was weak, but it gave her comfort. There were deep cracking noises coming from farther in the house where the walls and floors crumbled. And, almost inaudible through the fire's deep roar, was a voice.

Sophie opened her eyes and sat up, frowning. She could have sworn the voice had called her name. Then, a second later, it yelled, "Joseph!"

Garrett.

CHAPTER 34
FLIGHT

SUDDEN, PANICKY HOPE SENT Sophie stumbling to her feet. "Garrett! Down here!"

A figure appeared at the top of the stairs. It froze for a second to take in the scene then bounded toward them. Garrett's round, mustached face came into relief as he burst into the circle of light.

He pushed past Sophie to kneel by Joseph. He gave his nephew a light shake, pressed his fingers to Joseph's neck, and swore.

"Can you run?" he asked Sophie, and she nodded. "Good. I'll take Joseph. Stay close."

Garrett pulled Joseph's torso over one shoulder and lifted him. Sophie hovered beside them, shaking and terrified that the motion would be more than Joseph could endure. Garrett hitched his nephew higher then led the way back toward the stairs, glancing to each side as he moved.

"What the hell happened here?" he asked.

Sophie had neither the breath nor the presence of mind to explain the full story, but she said, "Destroying the house will kill the Grimlock."

Garrett made a small choking noise and stopped walking. "You're certain?"

"Mostly."

He took a deep breath and resumed climbing. His normally dull face twitched and spasmed as confusion, fear, and hope fought for dominance.

Sophie looked along the second floor as they passed it. She could see fire at the end of the hallway and even feel a little of its heat on her face. A crunching noise rolled through the building, and the stairs shivered under her feet.

Garrett moved quickly, and the bruises across Sophie's chest made it hard to match his pace, but she couldn't keep herself from asking, "How did you know where to find us?"

"Joseph slipped a note under my door, explaining what he was doing. I found it when the fire woke me."

"The fire—is the real house burning, too?"

"The real house," Garrett repeated, and a bitter smile flitted over his face. "Hah. They're one and the same building; the door just lets you see it with different eyes. But yes—Northwood is burning."

"Good," Sophie whispered, and Garrett gave her a proper smile.

She couldn't bring herself to look at Joseph. She had a horrible, overwhelming fear of seeing his face blank in death.

The only thing keeping her moving was the hope of getting him out of the house; if she lost that, she didn't think she could take another step.

"Where's Elise?"

"Outside."

"And Rose?"

"I couldn't find her."

The coldness in Garrett's voice was painfully familiar; it was the same tone Joseph had used when she'd first met him. *I can't believe I used to be so frightened of him.*

Fire had caught onto the left half of the stairs just before the third floor's landing. The flames licked across the wooden handrails and danced high above their heads. "Cover your face," Garrett said as he moved close to the stairs' right side.

The fire spat as they passed it, and the heat made Sophie squint. The temperature dropped once they reached the landing beyond it, though. The hallways were dark and cold; the fire hadn't yet spread to the third floor, though Sophie guessed it wouldn't take long. Garrett tightened his grip on Joseph and increased his pace to a brisk half jog as he took the left pathway. Sophie picked her skirts up and followed. She had to run to match Garrett's long strides, and she was soon breathless.

A scraping, hissing noise sent a shiver dancing up Sophie's spine, and she tugged on Garrett's sleeve to stop him. "There are corpses ahead."

He swore under his breath. "I don't have a gun. We'll take a different path."

They turned and retraced their steps past the stairs, where the fire was rapidly spreading. Barely five paces later, Sophie pulled on Garrett's sleeve again. "There are more this way."

With the fire contained to the lower levels, the cadavers on the third floor hadn't yet been infected by the flame. They writhed forward, spilling out of the blackness and into the golden glow, where they crouched, hissing. Garrett's face was white as he stepped backward. "We have to find a way through."

"There's so many," Sophie breathed. A dozen white, skull-like heads bobbed as they examined their prey, and scratching noises from farther in the hallway told her they weren't the only ones. In order for Garrett to fight them, he would have to drop Joseph— but that would anchor them to the one location and allow the corpses to encircle them. An idea hit her, and Sophie turned back to the stairwell. The flames had engulfed most of the railing, burning sections away and charring others. She found a post with live flames licking at its upper half, and pulled at its base. The wood was nearly hot enough to blister Sophie's hands, but it came free from the bracket with a scraping, crunching noise and a shower of embers.

"Keep behind me," Sophie said, putting herself between Garrett and the dead. Her hands shook as she aimed the post ahead of herself. "They hate fire. As soon as there's a gap, run."

"You'll follow?"

"Of course. Just get Joseph outside."

Garrett gave a small nod. Sophie moved a step closer to the cadavers, and they took that as an invitation to attack.

233

A cluster of the monsters swarmed toward her, empty eye sockets wide and toothy jaws gaping. Sophie gasped and arced the burning post across them. It glanced off two of the bodies without catching, but flames fizzled into life on the third. Sophie stumbled backward as the corpses hit her. There was nothing but noise, jostling, and snapping teeth for a moment, then shrieks split the air as the flames spread across the corpse. It tried to squirm away from the fire, and its companions clawed their way past it, unaware of the danger they were putting themselves in. Sophie stabbed at any that came close. Wails and hisses filled her ears as the flames spread across the cadavers and caught on the walls, as well.

Among the fear and adrenaline, Sophie felt a rush of relief at seeing the smothering red-and-gold wallpaper shrivel and blacken. Underneath was dry wood. The fire wouldn't take long to spread.

Light coursed down the hallway as the flaming creatures crashed into each other in their struggles. Garrett took advantage of their disorientation and charged through them like a bull. Sophie ran after him, waving her makeshift weapon blindly.

The noise was deafening. Flames burned her arms as she pushed past the dead. The toxic, billowing black smoke smothered her and stung her face, so Sophie closed her eyes and held her free hand ahead of herself to feel for walls or blockades. She tried to follow Garrett's footsteps, but there was so much pandemonium that she had to guess which direction they were leading her.

Bony hands grabbed at her, knocking her to the ground.

Sophie rolled onto her back and smacked one of the creatures away with the post before continuing to roll to get her feet under herself again. She hit a wall, unable to tell which direction she was supposed to face. When she opened her eyes, the black smoke reduced her visibility to almost nothing. Fire glowed to her left, so she turned right and continued running.

The smoke gradually cleared, and Sophie, gasping and choking, finally reached a part of the house where she could open her eyes and inhale clean air. Garrett was nowhere in sight.

She opened her mouth to call Garrett but thought better of it. Even if he was within hearing distance, calling would only attract more of the dead. The tip of her post had been reduced to embers. She didn't think it would be enough to light any more corpses—at least not easily—but she was reluctant to drop her only weapon.

Sophie turned on the spot, hoping she might recognize which section of the house she was in. To her eyes, it was identical to every other quarter. Even if she did stumble on a landmark such as the stairs or her room, it wouldn't help her escape. She needed to find the red door, but had no context for where it was. She'd only ever found it when she was desperately lost or had Rose's help.

Rose. A horrible, prickling sensation raised the hairs over Sophie's arms. She turned and inhaled sharply. Standing behind her, black hair a messy tumble about her shoulders and eyes so crazed that Sophie thought there might be almost nothing human left inside, stood Northwood's greatest believer.

CHAPTER 35
BLACK NIGHT

ROSE'S LIPS TWITCHED INTO a smile, but it was an insincere, reflexive expression. A glitter of something silver—a knife, Sophie guessed—hung loosely in her hand. "Are you lost, my dear?"

Something about Rose's voice was terribly wrong. Sophie thought the other woman might have been in shock—or she'd finally gone truly insane. She tightened her grip on the smoking post. "Did Joseph leave you a note, too?"

"Joseph?" Rose spoke as though she didn't know the name. Her dazed smile stretched wider, and her eyes roved over the hallway. "No. There's a fire, did you know? I came to save the house."

Sophie didn't speak, but she thought the house was a fair way past saving.

"There's something peculiar happening, though. This house has never caught fire before—not even when the chef drenched the floorboards in oil and lit them or when my great-uncle went insane and stacked firewood around its perimeter. The house is resilient, you see. It never decays. It never breaks. So how is it that, not even an hour after I show you to the red door, my home is being destroyed?" The rolling eyes fixed on Sophie and were abruptly filled with both presence and fury. "I'll kill you for what you've done."

Rose lunged. Sophie dove to one side, but slicing pain shot up her arm as Rose's knife caught her. Sophie shrieked and scrambled backward. The cut wasn't deep, but it hurt.

Completely dropping the genteel façade, Rose pivoted and lunged a second time. Animal fury twisted her face into something ugly and terrifying. She'd aimed the knife at Sophie's neck, and Sophie had barely enough time to swing the post in defense.

She wasn't strong enough to knock Rose away, but the post grazed Rose's hand and sent the knife skittering over the wooden floor. Rose landed on top of her, collapsing them both to the ground, and brought her nails across Sophie's face, clawing with almost inhuman strength.

Sophie thrashed, and her knee connected with Rose's stomach. Rose grunted and curled over, and Sophie kicked her away. A dribble of hot blood ran over her nose from where Rose's nails had scored her forehead, but Sophie was grateful she hadn't lost an eye. She got to her feet and pressed her back against the wall for support, breathing hard. Rose remained crouched on the ground. Blood mixed with frothing saliva ran from the corner of her mouth, but she didn't seem to notice as her bloodshot eyes bored into Sophie.

"You have no idea what you've wrought, child," she hissed. "You have no concept of what ruin you've brought on our great family."

"*Great family*," Sophie retorted. Her anger and fear made her speak recklessly. "There's no *great family* here—not anymore. All I see is a family that's decimated itself until the few survivors would greet death with open arms. You're the only one who can't understand how purely evil this house is."

"I'm the only one capable of understanding the privileges it bestows!" Rose bellowed. She threw herself forward, but Sophie was ready and swung the post with all of her strength.

Rose stumbled and dropped to her knees. She raised her hand and wiped a trickle of blood from the corner of her lips. "You've failed in your scheme to destroy us, child. We grew from one man. Now, this baptism by fire allows us to start with a clean beginning—to purge the doubters and the underminers from our descendants. The Shadow Being will appreciate my faithfulness; the Shadow Being will love me for my loyalty. He will give me many children. Northwood will be rebuilt from its ashes."

Sophie's eyes widened, and she took a step backward. She'd caught sight of something large moving through the smoky, shadowed hallway. Rose, too obsessed with her thoughts, had no awareness of their companion until the vast, black creature hit the wall beside her. The shock wave traveled through Sophie's bones and made her step away from it.

The Grimlock was dying. Its dried skin flaked away in large slivers, and its lamp-like eyes were flickering like a torch on the verge of fading. They passed over Sophie without any signs of recognition. It was gasping, and ropes of frothy saliva dripped from its open maw.

Rose stared at it in shock, then a hand fluttered to her chest as she exhaled, "It's *you*." Her eyes widened first in wonder then in adoration, and she crawled toward the Grimlock with groveling eagerness. "My lord, allow me to help you. Together we can still rebuild the Argenton family. Let us renew our ancient bargain."

The Grimlock swayed as its attention fixed on Rose. When it spoke, its voice had lost the previous, deep grating tones and sounded like dead leaves rattling together. "Ah, my dear Rose. I have not forgotten your loyalty. But your offer comes too late. The house is dead." A cruel smile twisted its face. "But there is still one way you can serve me."

Anticipation lit Rose's face, and her hands fluttered to touch the Grimlock's feet. "Anything, my lord."

The Grimlock's jaw stretched wide. Sophie turned away, too horrified to watch, as the teeth plunged into Rose's chest and sliced through flesh and bone.

Rose didn't even have enough time to scream.

The distant fire's roar fought to be heard over the snapping, crunching, sucking noises of the Grimlock eating. Without hesitation, Sophie fled down the hallway, desperate to escape the black creature before it noticed her.

The house was crumbling. Sophie turned onto a main hallway but had to retrace her steps as the floor ahead collapsed into a flaming pit. She had no idea which direction to take, or if she was heading toward danger or safety. The rising heat was unbearable, and the smoke choked her.

Something cold brushed Sophie's arm, and she gasped and jerked away from the sensation. She thought she could make out something faintly shimmering in the hallway. It looked like a heat mirage, but was gone a second later. Then the cold sensation returned to caress her other arm. Sophie turned, and cold sweat broke out across her body, despite the smothering heat. Then a voice whispered into her ear, "I'll show you the way to the red door."

"What—" Sophie breathed, but part of the ceiling collapsed behind her before she could phrase her question. *There's no time. If it says it will take me to the red door, I'll have to trust it.* "Show me."

An icy, invisible hand took hers and pulled her forward. It was a faint, transient sensation, like a puff of wind, and Sophie felt as though she could lose it if she squeezed too hard or moved too quickly. But the sensation drew her down the hallway, toward a door, which creaked open before they reached it.

They passed through the room and into the hallway on its other side then turned left. Sophie caught brief glimpses of more of the shimmering shapes—dozens, possibly even hundreds of them—shifting down the hallways and moving through the walls.

Sophie didn't dare speak it, but a suspicion was growing in the pit of her stomach. The corpses that littered the house were the physical representations of all who had died in Northwood.

What if these faint, cold shapes were the spiritual remains? Flesh and mind had been torn asunder; the Grimlock used the bodies, bending them to its will, while the souls remained trapped and powerless inside Northwood's walls.

But the walls were burning, and the spirits were being freed… and one of them wanted to help.

"We're close," the voice whispered. It was so faint, it almost felt as though it were spoken inside Sophie's mind. "Don't regret a single thing you did, miss. *I* don't."

Sophie turned toward the voice, and the shimmer flickered into clarity for the briefest fraction of a second. Warm brown eyes and a broad smile revealed themselves, and Sophie clasped a hand over her mouth. "Marie."

"Don't grieve for me," the spirit said. "You've set me free. I'm ready to move on, now. I can talk for the first time in my life. The others say the afterlife is a glorious place. I think I'll like it very much."

The hand pressed her own then faded. Sophie kept her fingers curled long after she knew she was alone. Tears stung her eyes and coursed down her cheeks. When she blinked them clear and looked up, she found herself facing the tall red door.

CHAPTER 36
MORNING

THE DIFFERENCE IN THE air was palpable when Sophie passed through the red door. She felt as though the atmosphere had cleared. Smoke still filled the hallways, but even that seemed less toxic than what had existed in the mirror house.

Sophie ached all over, and she was dizzy from lack of air, but she made herself run. The house was crumbling too quickly for her to stop and catch her breath; parts of the floor were collapsing behind her, sending up clouds of sparks and ash.

Strangely, though, the fire didn't frighten Sophie. It struck her as wholesome and cleansing: it was scorching away a toxic scar and returning the earth to a natural, neutral state.

Even though she was half-blinded by ash, gasping and coughing from the soot in her lungs, and so drained that her legs barely held her up, luck was on her side, and Sophie found her way to the stairs. Just like in the mirror house, they were half-burned away, but there was just enough intact railing for her to edge down one side until she reached the white-marble foyer.

The front doors stood wide open, and Sophie staggered to them with a dazed smile. The sun was rising. It hadn't yet reached the treetops, but the pink glow cast enough light for Sophie to see the gray-grass clearing. Dozens of figures huddled about the glade. The maids hung together in groups of twos and threes, sobbing quietly. The chef had collapsed to the ground and was chuckling to herself, and the butler stood watching the building burn with as much stately poise as he'd ever embodied.

Sophie followed the stairs to the grass, glad to leave Northwood for the final time. A few of the closest maids gave her watery smiles. Sophie returned the gesture, surprised and glad that the staff had finally met her eyes. She moved through the crowd quickly, scanning the figures with increasing desperation, until she found the two people she wanted to see more than anyone else: Garrett and Joseph.

Garrett had brought his nephew farther from the house than the staff had ventured and placed him near the lake. Neither man was moving; Joseph lay still, and Garrett knelt beside him, one hand pressed over his eyes.

Sophie broke into a run as cold terror choked her. *He can't be gone. We didn't go through all of that only to lose him.*

Joseph's face was corpse-white, and she couldn't tell if he was breathing. The fear combined with her exhaustion to drain her physically and mentally, and Sophie's run slowed to a walk as she neared the men.

Garrett looked up. Relief flashed over his face as he saw Sophie, and he held a hand toward her, beckoning her close. "You made it out—thank goodness. I thought you were behind me, but when I turned to check, you were gone. I tried to search for you, but the building was collapsing…" He sighed and shook his head. "I'm glad you're safe. Joseph never would have forgiven me if you'd been lost to the house."

Those last words sent hot, desperate hope through Sophie. She stumbled toward the men and dropped to her knees. "Joseph—is he—"

"Look for yourself." Garrett pulled aside Joseph's shredded shirt. To Sophie's shock and overwhelming relief, there were no open wounds. Instead, rivers of white scar tissue ran across his torso like frozen lightning.

Sophie stretched a shaking hand toward her husband. She ran her finger over one of the white marks in amazement, and Joseph's muscles twitched under her touch.

"It was eating him," she breathed. Fresh tears were threatening to spill from her, but she fought them back. "There was so much blood—"

"When you go through the red door, you're still within Northwood," Garrett said. "But it's a different *type* of Northwood. Things behave oddly and appear strange. The lamps in the foyer held blue, cold fire. Furniture disappears or is replaced by decayed versions of itself. You saw true: the creature mauled my nephew, but it damaged something other than his flesh. It was only in the *other* Northwood that it looked like blood."

"Will he be all right?"

Garrett sighed and leaned back to blink at the sky. "I hope so."

Sophie ran a hand over Joseph's forehead to push back the sooty black hair. He stirred and grimaced, and his eyes fluttered open before closing again.

"Do we have any water?" Sophie asked breathlessly. "Is the lake safe to drink from?"

Garrett nodded and stood.

Sophie continued to brush her hand over Joseph's face. His brow contracted then relaxed, and he opened his eyes and blinked at Sophie.

Tears created tracks down her dusty cheeks as relief mingled with anxiety, fear, and overpowering love made her shake.

"Sophie," Joseph croaked, and his hand moved toward her.

"Shh. You're safe. We're all right."

"Sophie," he gasped again and tried to sit. "You're hurt. You—"

Hysterical laughter bubbled through Sophie. She wiped the tears away from her face. "I'm fine. Don't struggle. Shh."

Joseph fought off her gentle pressure and pushed himself into a sitting position. His hand cupped Sophie's cheek as his eyes, darkly anxious, scanned her face and the blood running down her arm. His voice was tense and terrified. "What happened? How bad is it?"

"Not bad at all." Sophie had been trying to push Joseph to lie back down, but she gave up and let her hands linger on his chest. She could feel his heartbeat, strong and reliable, and it sent her own heart fluttering. "Don't move too fast. You're hurt. The Grimlock—I don't know what it did, but—"

Joseph followed her gaze to the white marks across his chest and frowned. "Well, that's unexpected. Though, I suppose, significantly better than the alternative."

Sophie couldn't decide if she wanted to laugh or cry, and she was embarrassed to find she was doing both. Joseph gently drew her closer and enveloped her in his arms.

"There, don't worry. You'll be all right. We'll get you to the doctor, and then we'll *both* be fine."

His hand began stroking her hair in the now-familiar gesture. Surprised to feel his fingers trembling, she tilted her head to see his face. There was so much intensity in his eyes that she found it impossible to look away.

"My dear Sophie. Whatever possessed you to go through the red door? You have no idea what it did to me to see the Grimlock standing over you. Promise you'll never put yourself in danger like that again."

"Only if you promise not to throw yourself into peril behind my back."

He gave her a weak smile. "I suppose I should apologize for that. But I knew you wouldn't have let me go willingly. Though I had expected you to be wise enough to leave Northwood once you were free to."

Sophie pressed her head back against Joseph's chest and closed her eyes. "I couldn't have gone while something so important was still inside."

Joseph kissed her hair and held her so tightly, she thought he might never let go. That was fine by her; his warmth felt good, and somehow he also smelled good, despite the smoke. She felt safe in his arms—safe from Rose, from the Grimlock, and from the house, which was gradually burning to the ground.

Garrett cleared his throat, and Sophie realized he had been standing a few feet away as he waited for their moment to finish. Elise, pale and agitated, stood at his side. Sophie felt herself turn red, but Joseph just laughed and beckoned his uncle and cousin to join them.

Garrett sat awkwardly and offered Joseph a flask, saying, "Water."

Sophie couldn't stop herself from stealing a glance at Elise. She was still pale, and dark circles rimmed her eyes, which she'd fixed on the house. Elise had been affected most by the Grimlock, but Sophie had hope that time would heal her.

Joseph pressed the flask into Sophie's hand, and she drank from it. The water was fetid, but because she was parched, it was one of the most delicious drinks she'd ever tasted. She took a mouthful then passed the flask back and followed Joseph's gaze to watch Northwood.

The vast structure had been entirely swallowed by flames, which rose higher than even the treetops and sent up a magnificent plume of black smoke. Sophie was almost certain she could see scores of tiny, shimmering shapes rolling through the smoke as the spirits departed the house.

Joseph kept his arm about Sophie, and she leaned her head against his shoulder. The air was cold, but even at their distance, she could feel the heat from the flames. Both Joseph and Garrett were silent. She tried to guess what they were feeling—relief, certainly, but she thought there was also some grief at the loss. They may have hated Northwood, but it had still been their home.

Sophie's thoughts turned to the missing family member, and she cleared her throat. As much as it hurt her to share the news, her family needed to know. "The Grimlock killed Rose."

Joseph's arm tightened around Sophie, but Garrett's expression didn't waver. He seemed to think for a moment, then said, "Perhaps that's the kindest end for her. Rose's life was so tangled with Northwood that I don't think she could have survived without it."

"It's still hard to believe it's gone," Joseph breathed. "We're *free*. What will you do, Garrett?"

"Hah." Garrett's mustache bristled. "I think I'd like to travel. I've never been far from this house, and Elise would benefit from experiencing more of the world. What about you?"

Joseph glanced at Sophie, and her heart fluttered at the affection in his eyes. "I'll go wherever Sophie takes me."

CHAPTER 37
DEPARTURE

THEY WATCHED THE FIRE for more than an hour. The building was far enough from the forest's perimeter that the flames couldn't reach the trees, and there wasn't any strong breeze to blow embers into the woods. Sophie didn't realize until later how lucky they'd been; if the forest had caught flame, none of them would have escaped.

Garrett was the first to rise. He moved among the staff, who had sat in small groups about the lawn to watch the house and talk in hushed tones, and counted their numbers.

Thanks to the butler, the entire staff had made it outside. Sophie heard the story in snatches. Apparently, Garrett's room wasn't far from where the first of the fire had taken hold, and he'd woken early. When he read Joseph's letter, he'd taken Elise to the butler then gone in search of his nephew. The butler had seen his young charge outside before returning to the house to rouse any of the staff who hadn't already woken. Thanks to his diligence, the worst injuries were a few minor burns and smoke inhalation.

The footmen had retrieved the horses and the carriage from the stables before the flames spread to it. One carriage wouldn't be enough to transport the staff from Northwood, though, and the town was too far for them to walk. Eventually, they decided that Joseph and Sophie, who both needed medical attention, would go first, along with four of the oldest staff.

They left not long after the sun topped the trees. The carriage was crowded, but Sophie didn't mind. It gave her an excuse to lean against Joseph. He kept his arm around her during the journey to town, and though his face was pale from the motion, he smiled whenever he caught her looking at him.

Once they reached town, Joseph hired rooms for them at the inn and summoned the doctor. Sophie had wanted Joseph to be treated first, but he left to arrange rescue parties to be sent for the remaining Northwood staff, leaving the doctor to stitch the knife wound on Sophie's arm and give her salve for the burns. Joseph didn't return until well after the doctor had left.

"We should call him back to look at you," Sophie said.

Looking exhausted, he kissed her cheek and stroked her sooty hair away from her face as he held her close. "Don't worry about me. I don't have any injuries to show him. You need rest, though."

"I need a bath more," Sophie mumbled into his shirt.

Joseph laughed. "Sometimes, I have trouble believing you're real." Sophie raised her head to frown at Joseph, and he enveloped her cheek in his palm and brushed his thumb over her skin.

"My darling, you're coated in blood and dirt, and there's so much ash in your hair that it appears gray. By all rights, you should look terrible, but I can't remember ever seeing a more enchanting woman."

Sophie couldn't smother her smile.

"I'm afraid we'll need to make do with the washbasin until we reach one of the larger inns in the next town," Joseph continued. "I ordered a clean dress, though, which should be brought in soon. I hope it fits. I had to guess your measurements."

Food arrived, and they ate quickly. Then Joseph left again to ensure a sufficient number of coaches and horses had been dispatched to Northwood. The day was passing quickly, and he couldn't allow any of the staff to remain at Northwood overnight—without shelter, they would freeze in the icy air.

Sophie washed up as best she could and changed out of the scorched, tattered dress. The gown Joseph had bought her was a sweet, floaty modern cut. She thought it was a little too pretty to be an appropriate emergency dress, but she appreciated that his taste was at least better than Rose's.

Her hair was too dirty to wash with just a pitcher of water, so she wrapped it up into a tight bun on top of her head.

Joseph had left her with instructions to sleep if she could, but she found it impossible to rest as long as he was away. She kept pacing between the window and the door, hoping to either catch a glimpse of Joseph or hear his footsteps on the stairs. He didn't return until late in the afternoon, and she felt her heart drop at his appearance.

He looked truly, thoroughly sick. His face was white, and he walked with a limp, but his warm smile returned when Sophie went to him.

"I promise you, I'm fine." His cheerful voice had a frightening thinness to it. "It's been a long day. The first of the Northwood party are arriving. They tell me the house's fire is nearly out. Northwood has been razed to the ground."

"Good," Sophie said.

"Were you able to sleep? You look tired."

"I couldn't. I'm too awake to even try."

"Well…" Joseph kissed her forehead, being careful to avoid the place where Rose's nails had scratched her. "We have a choice, then. The Northwood party will need lodging. I've spent today attempting to find accommodation wherever there's a spare room, but many families are so wary of Northwood that they won't take a single boarder. A handful of our staff will need to move on to the next town, which is another four hours away. You and I could spend the night here or be one of the first coaches to travel forward."

The more distance put between them and Northwood, the happier Sophie felt. Joseph agreed, and they left within the hour after paying for lodgings for the remaining staff. Joseph fell asleep in the carriage and slept through the night and much of the following day once they reached the next staging inn.

CHAPTER 38
HOME

IT WAS A GORGEOUS day. Rain from the previous evening had left the trees clean and crisp, and the sun was working to dry the mud and warm the air.

The weather reminded Sophie of her wedding day and how it had seemed almost too bright and pleasant. She felt worlds away from the terrified girl who had accepted Joseph's ring and whispered, "I will." She was strong, sure of herself and her choices, and truly happy in the knowledge that she'd accidentally married one of the best men in the country.

Joseph insisted the Grimlock hadn't caused any lasting damage, but his white scars still worried Sophie. He tired easily, and sometimes Sophie saw him flinch. He seemed to be gradually improving, though—he was more active each day, and his face was slowly regaining its color.

Sophie hoped she could convince him to let Uncle Phillip, the physician, examine him. Although Joseph had ensured Sophie had received the best medical attention available, he'd been reluctant to seek treatment for himself. The marks across his torso, though faded, would prompt questions that would be difficult to answer. If rumors started traveling through their peers that the Argentons had been engaging in witchcraft—or worse—it could make their future lives difficult. At least Sophie's uncle could be trusted to be discreet.

During their brief stops at the inns, Joseph spent much of his time hastily scribbling messages and calling on business contacts to arrange settlements for his staff. Most of the staff had spent their entire lives on the estate. Many had parents and even grandparents who had been given over to the Grimlock upon death. He felt the only right choice was to give them enough that they, too, could start a fresh life away from Northwood.

Their staff had scattered following Northwood's fall, and finding their addresses was proving difficult. The task consumed almost all of Joseph's time between the long hours of traveling and sometimes kept him up late into the night. The effort was draining him.

The only way Sophie could get him to rest was to say she herself felt tired. Then Joseph would drop everything else and sit with her, stroking her hair and arms while murmuring comforting words until they fell asleep together. At times like that, when she rested her head against Joseph's chest and listened to his steady heartbeat as his fingers stroked over her forehead, Sophie felt almost ashamed of how happy she was.

Joseph loved her. He made that so clear that she could never doubt it. He stole kisses when he passed her and made time for her when nothing else could distract him from his work, and when they held each other late at night, his eyes shone with such deep desire and affection that it took Sophie's breath away.

Their carriage pulled to a stop outside a narrow white house in the city. The flowering bushes in the front garden were full of blossoms, and the sun had done an admirable job of drying the water between the cobblestones. Joseph climbed from the carriage first, helped Sophie out, then threaded her arm through his.

"Ready?" he asked.

Sophie was too nervous and excited to reply, but she squeezed his arm in response. He chuckled, and together they climbed the stairs to the smart green door.

Their knock was answered quickly, and the housemaid, Anne, gasped and threw her apron over her face. She didn't even spare breath to greet them before turning back to the house in a flurry.

"Mr. Hemlock! Mr. Hemlock! Mrs. Argenton is here!"

Footsteps thundered through the house, then Sophie's father appeared in the doorway. They'd caught him early in the day. He needed a shave, and his hair was a messy tousle. He didn't seem capable of speaking, but the joy in his face told Sophie how much she'd been missed. He stretched his arms wide, and Sophie threw herself into them and hugged him tightly.

His eyes were wet when he finally pulled back, and he had to clear his throat before he could look at Joseph. He gave a brief nod, and Joseph replied with a gentle bow. "Sir."

"Well, you'd better come in." Sophie's father finally seemed able to control his voice as he patted Sophie's hand. "It's a little early for lunch—but why not. Let's have a meal brought in. Oh, my dear, I'm so glad you're home."

EPILOGUE

GARRETT ARGENTON SAT AT his writing desk, his pen poised over a clean page of paper. He'd never been good at words, and the letter he was trying to craft that morning was one of the hardest he'd ever had to write. It was necessary, though—horribly, crushingly necessary and becoming more so with every passing day.

He closed his eyes for a second. Then he lowered the pen to the paper and wrote the words that had been echoing through his head unrelentingly.

A quiet exhale made him look to his left, where Elise knelt on the floor. Her eyes were vacant as she drew the charcoal across the paper. She was surrounded by a halo of hundreds of sheets, all showing the same figure with its inky black body and its jaws stretched open. Lamp-like eyes stared out of the drawings with furious, ravenous intensity.

Garrett looked back at his letter, where he'd written four simple words.

Joseph,

It's not dead.

**The haunting is far from over.
See the conclusion to Sophie's story in
House of Secrets, available now.**

CHAPTER 1
MOONLIT

SOPHIE WAS TRAPPED INSIDE the smothering red-and-gold hallways. The walls seemed to grow impossibly high to either side, and her breath plumed in the icy air as she scuttled away from the huge, dark shape that stalked her. It opened its vast black jaws, and ropes of saliva dropped onto the wood floor.

"No!" Sophie shrieked. Her back hit something solid, and she looked up. The red door was to her back, but its handle was far too high to reach.

Somewhere in the distance, Joseph screamed. He'd been torn open by the beast, and there was nothing she could do to save him. She couldn't even hold his hand and comfort him as he bled out.

The Grimlock reached its claws toward her face. Its maw stretched wide, and she could smell its fetid, rotting breath as it prepared to tear her in two.

Sophie screamed. The Grimlock's hands squeezed her, and she thrashed to pull free. But instead of feeling the sharp, cutting pain of teeth, Sophie realized she was struggling against something soft and giving. She opened her eyes and sucked in rapid, panicked breaths.

She was in her room. It was dark, but the coals in the fireplace still glowed, and the air was crisp, telling her it must be early morning.

She rolled onto her side to feel for Joseph's comforting warmth, but his half of the bed was empty. Dream and reality bled together for a second, and Sophie struggled to her feet, heart fluttering, as she prepared to search the labyrinthine Northwood for her husband.

No. Northwood was burned to the ground. It can't touch us any longer.

Sophie sank back onto the edge of her bed. The icy air sent chills through her as she gazed about the room.

She and Joseph had come directly to her father following their escape from Northwood, and they were staying at his city house until they could secure a property of their own. While the building wasn't tiny, it had a limited number of rooms, and Sophie and Joseph were sharing her old bedroom, which was still decorated in powder blue with bronze trimmings.

Sophie was glad to have her husband's company at night, but she couldn't stop the creeping worry that her feeling wasn't reciprocated. Every morning during the past week, she'd woken alone.

She tried to tell herself that Joseph was simply an early riser, but the sun hadn't yet breached the skyline, and when Sophie turned toward the window, she could make out a myriad of barely visible stars.

He's avoiding me. Sophie's hands were still shaking from the nightmare. She squeezed them together to keep them still and tried to slow her breathing. *But when we left Northwood two weeks ago, he loved me. I was so sure of it. I couldn't have misread his intentions, could I?*

"No." The word seemed to hover in the lonely room. *He told me he loved me. Once.*

Unable to sit any longer, Sophie rose and pulled her gown around her shoulders. The fireplace's glow was strong enough to show that Joseph's coat and hat no longer sat on the chair where he'd placed them the night before. That meant he'd gone out rather than simply moving to a different room in the house. Sophie crossed to the window and squinted at the ghostly shimmers of light that caught on the rooftops and cobblestones and hovered amid the fog. The street was undisturbed by man or beast.

It's not safe out at night. The only people still awake would slit Joseph's throat for his money.

Sophie squeezed her eyes closed and gripped the windowsill so tightly that her fingers ached. *No, he'll be safe. He's not foolish, and he can defend himself if it comes to that. But why did he go out so early? Did he have trouble sleeping, or did he want to be alone?*

A faint tapping made Sophie open her eyes. The sound came from the street below, but it echoed between the houses and made

Sophie unsure of its direction. Just as the noise resolved itself into brisk footsteps, a figure swept into view, its long legs gliding through the tendrils of mist. Sophie recognized the posture and quick pace as her husband's, and the band of anxiety around her chest loosened.

She turned from the window, intending to go downstairs and greet him at the door, but stopped herself. *He left so that he could be alone. Don't smother him; wait for him to come back to you.*

Sophie shed her gown and slid back into the bed. She listened to the downstairs door close with a muffled click, then she heard footsteps move through the foyer. She stayed awake for hours until the sun rose and dispelled the fog and the house was filled with the maids' footsteps and voices, but Joseph didn't rejoin her.

CHAPTER 2
BREAKFAST

SOPHIE SPENT LONGER THAN normal on dressing that morning. Joseph had once told her he liked her light-gold hair. She'd had her maid recreate a style she'd seen on a fashionable woman in town and weave tiny fake flowers through it. The style was more appropriate for an afternoon out than breakfast, but she didn't care about impressing the city's elite. She only wanted one man's notice.

By the time she hurried downstairs, the early-morning bustle had faded. Sophie's father, Mr. Hemlock, had left early for an appointment with his lawyer. Sophie was half-afraid that Joseph might have gone out too, but she found him in the breakfast room, reading the newspaper while he sipped tea.

"Good morning." Sophie moved toward the serving table and helped herself to cold meat and toast. "Did you sleep well?"

Joseph looked at her. Sophie felt a small spark of joy as his eyes flicked to her hair, but her triumph was crushed when he immediately returned his attention to the paper. "Yes, thank you."

"I'm glad." Sophie sat opposite her husband and furtively examined him. His pitch-black hair and dark eyes contrasted sharply with his pale skin. Sophie had always found his angled features deeply attractive, but his cheeks were a little too sunken for her to be happy about his health. The Grimlock, the creature that had inhabited their old home and had bound the Argenton family to its ancient bargain, had injured Joseph before they'd escaped. The only remnants of that battle were a myriad of ice-white scars across his torso and a lingering gauntness. *He's still healing,* she reminded herself. *Uncle Phillip has been treating him, and there's no one I would trust more to care for Joseph.*

Sophie picked at her food as she struggled to find a way to break the silence. "Is there any interesting news?"

Again, she earned herself a brief glance before he returned to the paper. "Not today. A theft. Scandals. A fire that was contained before it could spread. Nothing that affects us."

"Well…I suppose I prefer dull news to bad news."

This time Joseph's eyes met hers and stayed there. A smile flickered over his lips. "Yes, I suppose I do too." He didn't speak for a moment before murmuring, so quietly that Sophie wasn't sure she was supposed to have heard, "You look beautiful."

Sophie couldn't stop the heat from spreading over her face. She beamed and knotted her hands in the folds of her dress as her heart jumped. His smile, his words, the warmth in his eyes—she felt as though she'd been transported back to the days following the Grimlock's defeat, when Joseph's affection had been unguarded and generous. "I—"

A door above them slammed, followed by a shriek of laughter from Sophie's younger brother and a hushed scolding from the governess. The noise intruded like a knife cutting them apart, and Joseph turned to his newspaper with the same indifferent expression he'd worn when she'd entered the room. Their brief moment might as well have not existed.

Sophie tried to swallow the disappointment as she returned to picking at her breakfast. *Is there something wrong with him? Have I made him unhappy? Or is it this house? I can't imagine him wanting to live with my family for much longer. Yet he still hasn't raised the subject of moving. Has he already started looking for a suitable property, or would he tell me first?*

As Sophie examined the man opposite her, she was struck with the unsettling sensation that she was watching a stranger. They'd been married for barely three weeks, and most of their first days as husband and wife had been muddied with secrets and lies. Following Northwood's destruction, they'd shared a brief euphoric period when Joseph had kissed her eagerly and kept her awake late into the night. But within days of their return to her father's house, his attentions had stopped.

She'd spun through every excuse she could find. *He's not used to the bustle of the city, and it's exhausted him; he's recovering from his injuries; he's still coming to terms with the change in circumstances; he's grieving his aunt's death; he misses his uncle and cousin.*

But as the days passed and Joseph showed no symptoms of

stress, pain, or loneliness, Sophie had been forced to turn to more distressing options: the source of his discontent was either their house...or her.

You were a fool to think he would love you, a cruel little voice whispered in the back of her mind. *It was a loveless marriage; what did you expect the result to be—that you would defy the odds and find a partner who would reciprocate your feelings? Stop being naïve. He needed a wife to sacrifice to the Grimlock. He chose you on a whim. And now that he's free from the beast, he's begun to regret his decision.*

"Have you thought about where we should move?" The words escaped her in a desperate rush, and her insides turned cold from embarrassment. Sophie hadn't intended to speak so brashly or quickly.

Joseph looked up. "I'm pleased to stay here as long as your father welcomes us."

"Oh." Sophie tried to place her cutlery on the plate but released the fork too soon and grimaced at the sharp clatter. She cleared her throat. "I thought...I..."

Joseph folded the paper and set it to one side. He clasped his hands on the table and leaned forward so that Sophie couldn't avoid his gaze. Although the force of his attention was unnerving, his voice was soft. "Go on."

"It might be nice...to be established in our own house..."

Joseph let the silence stretch until Sophie began to worry she'd made the situation worse. Then he said with no discernible emotion, "If you like."

Is he annoyed? Did I speak out of turn?

Sophie opened her mouth, floundering for some words to ease the tension, but was spared having to speak when the housekeeper entered the room in a bustle of thick skirts. "Begging your pardons, but a letter has arrived for Mr. Argenton. Express."

Joseph's eyebrows drew together as he held out his hand for the note. The housekeeper passed it to him, bobbed a curtsy, and left. Joseph was silent as he broke the letter open and read.

Sophie tried to guess his thoughts. They clearly weren't pleasant. His expression hardened, his lips tightening and his brow lowering until he was glowering at the paper. A strange intensity entered his eyes. Not for the first time, he reminded Sophie of a wild animal barely contained behind a veneer of civility.

She couldn't read the contents, but she could see that the note was short. Joseph read it twice before dropping it to the table and lacing his hands under his chin.

"Well, my dear," he said at last. His voice, raw and cold, sent chills through Sophie. "It seems we will not escape today without bad news after all."

ABOUT THE AUTHOR

Darcy Coates is the *USA Today* bestselling author of *Hunted*, *The Haunting of Ashburn House*, *Craven Manor*, and more than a dozen other horror and suspense titles. She lives on the Central Coast of Australia with her family, cats, and a garden full of herbs and vegetables. Darcy loves forests, especially old-growth forests where the trees dwarf anyone who steps between them. Wherever she lives, she tries to have a mountain range close by.